ALSO BY Y. BLAK MOORE

Triple Take

The Apostles

SLIPPING

Y. BLAK MOORE

SLIPPING

A NOVEL

ONE WORLD

BALLANTINE BOOKS / NEW YORK

A One World Books Trade Paperback Original

Published in the United States by One World Books, an imprint of The Random House Publishing Group, a division of Random House, Inc., New York.

One World is a registered trademark and the One World colophon is a trademark of Random House, Inc.

ISBN 0-7394-5818-3

Printed in the United States of America

Book design by Casey Hampton

To my daughter Cacharel. The sight of your pretty brown face and innocent but knowing eyes as an infant made me want to get clean.

To my daughter Ciara. You're too much like your doggone mama, but I won't hold that against you.

To my "sun," Yanier. Hopefully you won't follow my misguided path to get to where you want to be in life.

To my Number 1, Akilah. You held me down like free lunch and I love you for that. Keep checking for me 'cause I'll keep checking for you.

To my pops, Franklin Moore. You lost your life to your drug addiction long before you had a chance to see me grow into a man. I hope that you would have loved me as I love my "sun." It has taken decades but I have finally learned to forgive you, if only because of my own experience with mind- and mood-altering chemicals.

To every last one of y'all out there slaving day in and day out to try to quiet those cravings for narcotics to medicate your tired souls in this land of less-than-nothings and defeated underdogs.

SLIPPING

PROLOGUE

DUSK SETTLED ON THE VERMIN-INFESTED TENEMENTS OF Chicago's ghettos. Nightfall may bring peace to the inhabitants of suburbia, but the darkness that covers the inner city serves to uncloak its vampires, the living dead that feed on one another for sustenance. Death accompanied the darkness like an uninvited party guest. In ghettos all around the globe many won't survive the deadly darkness. Some will cross the void at the hands of a trigger-happy robber, others will succumb to the poison of narcotics, still others will fall victim to the knife of a spurned lover.

In the morning the so-called authorities will try to patch up the ghetto's wounds. In an attempt to pacify the so-called community leaders they will dispatch their brand of justice, but only in the daylight hours. They know that the night belongs to the vampires. Furtively, outraged and upstanding citizens will assist the authorities in their misguided, ignorant efforts to mete out punishment. With impunity they rule the daylight hours trying to repeal the ghetto's madness, but they know they have only a few short hours before the streetlights blink on again, signaling the return of the vampires.

As the sun was swallowed by the darkness, a forlorn figure sat on the floor of a sagging, gutted-out tenement. The young man was dirty and disheveled. Besides the filthy clothes on his body, his only worldly possessions were spread about before him: a glass crackpipe, four cigarette lighters, a Baggie containing an ounce of crack cocaine, and a chrome .357 Python with a wicked gleam to it. These meager articles were the cornerstone of his lowly existence. He was a hype, geeker, clucker, crackhead, or whatever the current ghetto terminology was for being addicted to the all-consuming drug crack. He seemed more dead than alive, and if not for his sparse movements and the tortured sighs that escaped him every so often, one would have thought that he had already passed from this realm. Donald "Don-Don" Haskill was a wanted man, if you could call him a man. His age didn't make him a man, only the horrors he'd seen and had perpetrated granted him that boon. Several irate groups of people were scouring his old stomping grounds in search of him. He had been hiding in this apartment for close to three days. The last bit of food that had crossed his lips was a candy bar more than two days ago. He was so thirsty he had been contemplating drinking out of the rusty toilet in the bathroom. The only thing that deterred him was the smell of the rotted water and the fear of ingesting maggots.

Depression blanketed him as he thought of the circumstances that led up to his present dilemma. He heaved himself up from the floor and walked over to the window. He stared out of the broken, dirty panes at the inky shroud of darkness settling over the city. Finally he reached a decision. He glanced at the luminescent dial of his cheap wristwatch. He would make his move soon. Gathering his things, he inspected his handgun. A feeling of companionship flooded his soul as he held the pistol. Through all of his escapades it had been his best friend—more faithful than any woman, more steadfast than any friend. Unlike fickle semiautomatics, his Python had never let him down. Even now, when he had been neglecting his appearance and hygiene, his revolver remained clean, well oiled, and shiny.

Don placed the pistol within arm's reach on a tattered piece of cloth on the floor and reached for his crack. He pinched a piece from the bag and placed it on the screen of his pipe. Using his cigarette lighter, he touched the flame to the piece of crack and allowed it to melt the white-yellow rock, and then he inhaled the effervescent smoke. After he expelled the smoke from his nose he coughed until he hacked up a ball of yellowish mucus. With a mighty whoosh he expelled the ball of phlegm across the room. It made a slapping sound on the wall ten feet away. The superfast effect of the crack relaxed and tightened his entire body and he leaned back against the wall and replayed the events that led him here.

"DONALD HASKILL, GET YO LAZY BUTT UP AND GET READY for school! Don-Don, you heard me, get yo raggedy, nappy-head butt up!"

"I'm up, I'm up. Quit hollering like a fool!" Don answered grumpily.

"No you ain't, yo lazy butt! Don't make me come up there and throw some cold water on yo funky butt!"

Ignoring his sister's last remark, he asked, "Ay, girl, is Momma gone?"

"Boy, yeah. Momma been gone since six o'clock this morning. She waited for you to come in till one o'clock last night. She said to tell you to start bringing yo butt in this house at a decent hour. Just because she be spending time over her boyfriend house, she said to let you know that you only seventeen and you better start coming in this doggone house at a decent time on school nights."

Don cut her off. "Did she leave me some money?"

His sister left the bathroom and climbed the few stairs to Don's bedroom door, opened the door wide, and leaned on the doorjamb.

She gloated, "She left me some money, but she didn't leave you any. She would have, but you weren't here. She said that she would have had to stop at the cash station and get some out and she wasn't going to go through all of that trouble for you and you weren't even here. If you stopped hanging out in the streets with them no-good friends of yours and got you a little part-time job or something after school then you wouldn't have to wait on Momma to give you money all the time. I got to get ready for school. Something you should be concerning yourself about."

As Rhonda retreated to finish preparing to leave, Don chuckled at his sister's short speech. He loved Rhonda and he knew that she loved him, but she seemed to hate all of his friends and told him so at every available opportunity. She was nineteen, two years his senior, but she thought she was thirty. Because their mother worked long, hard hours as a Chicago policewoman, attended college, and still tried to have some semblance of a love life, Rhonda stepped up to play the role of surrogate mother to the hilt. He had to admit, she did manage to take pretty good care of home base with his mother being gone so much. She even looked like their mother, especially when she was fussing at him.

Don couldn't remember much of his father, outside of his death, but his aunts and uncles claimed that he was the spitting image of the man. Whenever the subject of his old man arose his mother became tight-lipped. From what information he had been able to piece together about his father, his story was the same as too many Black men in America. Systematically raped and dehumanized by the unholy caste system in America, his father turned to the bottle. After four years of diligent service in the army, then as a glorified janitor at city hall, he grew tired of being overlooked for promotions. He thought no one at work noticed his deepening depression. The last day of his life he appeared to be happier than he had been in years. He whistled a cheery tune all day as he completed his daily tasks. When his coworkers noticed his obvious attitude adjustment and questioned him about the change, his only reply was a smile that seemed to signify that he had a secret—a secret that tickled him pink. At quitting time he cheerfully bid everyone farewell. At home he ate the dinner his wife had thoughtfully prepared in between her job as a loss-prevention specialist at Marshall Field's downtown on State Street and her classes at Kennedy King Junior College. He drank two beers as he watched the evening news and then he took his .38 caliber handgun out of the closet, climbed to the roof of their apartment building, sat on a milk crate placed against the brick chimney, and ate a bullet.

On the roof, with a large portion of his head missing, is where Don-Don found his father. He had done his best to make several airplanes from notebook paper and took them to the roof to launch them with his dad. His four-year-old mind couldn't contemplate the blood and brain matter splattered on the bricks behind his dad, so he shook his father's shoulder to tell him to get up and help him fly his airplanes. His father's lifeless body sprawled forward and pinned Don to the rooftop. As blood and goo oozed from his father's mouth and head onto Don's face, he began screaming, and when help finally came, that was how they found them.

At first Don's mother didn't think she could live without his father. After all, he was her first love and the father of both of her children. When she first found out that she was pregnant with Rhonda, she thought that he would back out on her, but he married her and put his dream of becoming a musician on hold. Instead he did the honorable thing and went off to join the army to support his family. On one of his home passes he planted Donald in his wife, when Rhonda was eighteen months old. During his years in the service he appeared to be reasonably faithful and after his honorable discharge he returned home and got a job. For a while he tried to hang out with his musician buddies, but their drug abuse, womanizing ways, and general lack of responsibility made him, a faithfully married, employed father of two, a stranger among them.

After her husband's suicide, it almost made Hazel want to take her own life, just knowing that the man she loved with all her heart was going through enough mental anguish to make him take his own life, but he hadn't confided in her. The thought of their two kids allowed her to draw from the reserve strength all Black mothers seem to have to continue on with her life. Using the money from her husband's meager life-insurance policy, she purchased a small house in Chicago's West Woodlawn area, at the time a middle-working-class neighborhood, and an old jalopy to get back and forth to her job. A few years later she took the city policeman's test and passed it with flying colors and joined the force. Over the years she found herself increasingly overprotective of Don. She would scrutinize his every mood and give in to his every need. She hadn't dated seriously for close to a decade of her children's lives, and even now that she had a new boyfriend, a Cook County sheriff's deputy, she wouldn't really allow him around her children. She had recently returned to school to earn her master's degree so she could take the lieutenant's exam. With the hours Don kept, he rarely seemed to see his mother except on her days off. Whenever he did manage to bump into her, their face-to-face encounters usually ended up in shouting matches spanning everything from his grades to his street life to his blatant disregard for house rules.

"Damn, I needed a few dollars too," Don said as he put his feet on the floor.

He flinched at the cool wood on his bare soles. His young bones creaked as he bent over to pick up the pair of pants he'd worn the previous day. Out of the hip pocket he fished half of a blunt. He straightened up and looked in the large mirror on top of his dresser. He saw a brown-skinned boy just a shade away from being a man; standing at five foot ten and weighing 173 pounds he wasn't really skinny, but he wasn't heavy either. He didn't have six-pack abs, but there wasn't any flab around his middle. His short fade sported a few waves on the top, but they weren't really defined because he didn't have the patience to sit and brush his hair hour after hour. Strong peach fuzz was evident around his mouth and under his chin, complementing his strong facial features. With a heavy sigh he lit the tip of the blunt with his lighter and took a long pull. He held the smoke in his lungs until he choked. For his efforts he was rewarded by the instant euphoric effects of the weed on his system. With his sister in mind he walked down the short hallway to the top of the staircase.

He called, "Rhonda! You want to hit this shit! It might mellow yo high-strung ass out some!"

"I don't think so. You don't even need to be smoking that stuff in the house! I don't even see how you smoke that mess so early in the damn morning! That's all you little dummies spend every cent you get your hands on! I'm leaving you ten dollars on the table. I've got to go. I can't be late for humanities because of you. Make sure you take your behind to school too!"

The front door slammed as he headed for the bathroom. He pulled his boxers down and perched on the white porcelain toilet. Leisurely he thumbed through a *Sports Illustrated* magazine while he smoked and obeyed nature's order to put out the garbage. He wondered what was on the agenda for the day. He had to laugh at that thought. He already knew the answer—the same as every other day. Ditching school, hanging out, dodging the police, trying to come upon money for weed and alcohol, and trying to talk some young girl out of her panties. Even though it was a school day, attending was definitely out of the question. He hadn't been to school in two months. School was for the winter time. It was spring.

After showering and dressing, he devoured half of a box of Cap'n Crunch and left the house. His first stop was Momma Taylor's weed spot on Vernon, the best weed in the neighborhood. Momma Taylor had the biggest bags and the best green that could be bought for ten dollars. After his purchase he ducked into the first unlocked hallway he came to and rolled two blunts. He dumped the contents of the cheap cigars on the carpeted steps of the hallway. He slid one of the blunts into the top of his sock and pulled his pant leg back down. He lit the other as he relaxed on the stairs. He smoked about half of the blunt before putting it out and sliding it into the band of his Los Angeles Dodgers baseball cap.

He then headed to the pool hall. Confidently he pushed open the door and stepped inside. He began to greet his boys.

"Li'l Joe, what's up, nigga? Damn, Semo, who cut yo hair? Want me to whup his ass for you? Tabo, yeah, nigga. Don't pretend like you don't see me, nigga. What's up wit my ten dollars? You always trying to act like you broke. We gone fall out about that little money."

Happy that the whole gang was there, Don exchanged a few more playful remarks while he settled into the atmosphere. No sooner had he deposited a quarter into a video game than a light-skinned, wavy-haired boy stepped over to join him by the game.

"Double-D, what's up, nigga?" the boy greeted him happily.

Glancing over his shoulder, Don continued to fight off the demons in the video game as he replied, "Dre, what the deal, baby boy? What you niggas get into when I left last night? I was so fucked up, I don't even remember going to the crib."

"Don, yo ass missed it! After you broke it out last night, we was laying back, niggas sleep and shit, then Gail and her ugly-ass sister came through."

"Gail?"

"Big-nose Gail, that got that ugly-ass sister that so damn thick. Man we got to pouring gin in them hoes. That do-it fluid got them bitches hot and it was on."

"What you mean?"

Dre pulled an imaginary train whistle cord. "Choo, choo."

"Get yo lying ass outta here!" Don said, not wanting to believe that he had missed out on the main event.

"Nigga, I ain't lying. We all hit them bitches. Jag, Carlos, Keno, and Big Man. I hit both of them. Gail wouldn't suck no dick, though. Her ugly-ass sister was trying to but it felt like she had a mouth full of razor blades. And guess what?"

"What, nigga?" Don asked as he slapped the buttons and joystick.

"Nigga, you just salty cause you missed out on that pussy," Dre said.

"Whatever, nigga," Don scoffed. He lied, "I ain't salty 'bout no big-nose Gail and her ugly-ass sister. I can get both of them bitches if I wanted to. Now fuck all that. What was you finta say?"

"Oh yeah. After we all had a couple of go-rounds wadn't no more rubbers and shit, right? Man, this nigga Jag get to searching like crazy for a rubber. Everybody telling him ain't no more, right. This thirsty-ass nigga get to hitting Gail raw. We tripping on this nigga, right. Most of us ain't hitting shit raw, 'specially after that little runner Miesha damn near burnt our dicks off last summer."

"You ain't lying," Don agreed as he thought about the severe pain he experienced as he urinated one morning three days after he and his friends ran a train on Miesha. "That girl had me leaking like a broken faucet."

"Right, right. Well, by this time, Gail was passed out anyway. She stretched out on the couch with her mouth wide open and Jag is running up in her. Just when he 'bout to nut he jump up with his pants around his ankles and aims for her mouth. When he jumped up, Gail woke up and as he aiming for her face she move. He trying to move with her and tripped on his pants. Anyway, to make a long story short, he missed and Semo was salty than a motherfucker. Enough of that shit, though. I just came from yo crib trying to catch you. I got business to discuss."

"What kind of business you got to discuss, Mr. Porno Star?" Don asked, his voice dripping with envy.

Dre ignored his friend's salty attitude. "Guess who I hollered at yesterday?"

"I don't know."

"Guess, man."

Don exploded. "Nigga, quit playing that twenty questions shit and tell me what the fuck you talking about!"

"Awight, don't get yo panties in a bunch. Yesterday I was shooting ball with Diego and them up at Harper Court. Them niggas think they can hoop. They was talking shit like they was so cold and shit. I told them niggas to stick to selling drugs 'cause we would come through there and spank they ass hooping. Niggas trying to hoop with new-ass clothes on and jewelry and shit. That shit be funny seeing them niggas trying to stay clean and play ball at the same time. Man . . . ."

"Excuse me, Dre, would you get to the fucking point!"

Dre rolled his eyes to the ceiling. "Anyway. We argued for awhile and it all boiled down to they say they would play us any time for any amount. Them niggas know we ain't making no paper or nothing, so they say that they would triple any amount of money we came up with. They was talking so much shit it wadn't even funny. All the time they woofin', I won two games of varsity going up to 31."

Don released the video game's joystick and slapped Dre in the back of the head.

"Why the fuck didn't you tell me that shit last night," he fumed.

"I was high than a motherfucka, I forgot all about shit," Dre answered, rubbing the back of his head.

Grabbing the joystick again, Don continued to play the video game. He said, "Dre, you'se a ignorant motherfucka if I ever seen one. You don't use yo gotdamn brain at all." Don fell silent as he concentrated on his game and searched his brain for a way to get hold of a lot of money fast. Dre chattered incessantly in his ear, but over the years Don had learned to ignore his talkative friend when necessary. Sensing that Don was scheming, Dre was just about to walk away when he spoke.

"Dre, is yo big brother still slinging all that dope in the Wells?" Don asked.

"Yeah. Why?"

"Do that nigga still hide his money in y'all basement?"

Apprehensively Dre nodded his head up and down. He could tell from the look on Don-Don's face that he was getting another one of his infamous brainstorms—and that usually meant trouble.

"Run to the crib and get a gee, I'll round up the fellas," Don ordered.

"Damn, a thousand dollars, man. I don't know about that shit. What if we lose that shit? My brother would kill me. You know that nigga be sweating about pennies and shit. Always crying broke. Then them nigga at the court could get on some bullshit. What if them niggas don't want to pay us if we win?"

"Dre, my nonbeliever of a friend, we don't plan on losing. You know that them niggas can't do shit with us on no basketball court. Ain't a nigga that be with them that can play no ball for real. And if they try not to pay us after we beat they ass, I'll kill one of them studs. Now quit asking all them damn questions and go get that paper; Imma take care of everything. We'll have them ends back before you brother know it's gone."

Don's silver tongue managed to put Dre's fears to rest, so he hastily exited the pool hall to filch the money from his brother's stash. Don lost the last man on his video game. While the word *continue* flashed on the screen, he dug in his pockets to try to find another quarter, but he didn't have one.

"Oh well," he said as he looked around the pool hall and began calling the names of his friends. "Keno, Carlos, Big Man, y'all check it out. Y'all want to make some quick money doing what we do best?" he asked when the three youngsters were within earshot.

"Don-Don, you ain't even got to ask us no stupid shit like that," Big Man drawled in his usual countrified manner.

Don said, "Alright. Just hold tight til Dre come back, then we gone go over to Harper Court and shoot the lights out them niggas that run with Diego."

Excited at the prospect of easy money, the small group

exited the pool hall. They sat on garbage cans in the mouth of a nearby alley for shade from the glowing midday sun. Don took off his hat and pulled the half of blunt from the headband of his fitted cap. He lit it and took a few puffs, then passed it to his friends. Dante was the first among them to choke. They laughed at their friend as he gagged and spit with tears in his eyes. Dre ran past them headed for the pool hall.

"Yo, Dr. Dre! Dre!" Don yelled.

Dre backpedaled and peeked into the alley. He had to shield his eyes so that he could see his friends clearly. His right hand was shoved into the pocket of his jeans like he was holding on to something extremely valuable.

Don asked, "Did you get it?"

Breathlessly Dre nodded his head.

Don jumped down from the garbage can. He addressed the troops. "C'mon y'all. Let's go hit these niggas up for this paper. I'm telling y'all, when we get out here don't be playing no games with these studs. Don't underestimate 'em either. The minute we start playing them studs like they sweet, they can sneak up and get a win. Don't be on no soft shit neither. If we got to fight for every loose ball and every call we on that shit. If they want to throw they hands up, then we gone be some fighting motherfuckers 'cause we here to get this paper. Y'all got it?"

Everybody agreed.

Lighthearted at the prospect of winning some easy

money, the five friends started the short journey to Harper Court. They were all in a good mood except Dre, who couldn't think about having a good time until his big brother's money was safely back in its hiding place in the basement. When they reached Harper Court they saw Diego and his usual band of flunkies, selling drugs and shooting baskets. The basketball court was a front for the dealers to sell their merchandise under the guise of being avid sports competitors. The five boys walked through the gate and stepped onto the court. Diego was sitting on a bench with a couple of girls who looked too young for him to be hollering at, but he was leering at them like they were supermodels.

Don called out to him. "Diego, what's up, yo? Let me holla at choo."

Diego left the bench and met Don and his crew in the middle of the court.

Jerking his thumb in Dre's direction, Don said, "My nigga told me that y'all studs was up here talking crazy 'bout what you would do to us on the court. It sound like you studs want to donate some of that drug money."

"You ain't said shit slick," Diego said. "We right here, we got a ball and we standing on a court."

"Whoa, pimp. Slow it down. I seem to remember my man telling me something about three-to-one odds. It sounded to me like you was just woofin'. Ain't that right fellas? 'Cause I know you ain't got no paper like that."

Even though Diego didn't have as much money as he pretended, there was no way that he could let Don and his crew, or his own cronies, know that. That information could damage his reputation and people would stop treating him like he was big-time. Besides, he knew that Don and his boys couldn't have that much money anyway. He knew that they didn't serve or work regular jobs, so how much scratch could they have gotten hold of? He decided to call Don's bluff.

"Yeah, nigga, I said it. I ain't biting my tongue neither. Let me see yo money, frontin'-ass nigga."

Whipping out the thousand dollars, Don offered the money to Diego to count. Diego eyed the deceivingly thin bankroll but refused to touch it. He tried to guess the amount of bills hidden from his view by the ten-dollar bill on top. It looked to him like it couldn't have been more than fifty bucks.

Diego laughed. "You niggas come up in here acting like y'all got big paper. We can play for that little shit. I'll give y'all five-to-one odds."

Don and his friends joined in Diego's laughter. Turning to the growing crowd of curious onlookers, Don said, "Y'all heard the wetback, right? He said that he gone give us five-to-one odds. For all of y'all that failed math or just don't know shit, that mean for every one dollar we got, he gone put up five dollars."

With a puzzled look on his face, Diego watched Don's strange antics. He was starting to feel uneasy, but it was too late. Ever since grammar school the two boys had competed at everything from getting girls to sports, from basketball to pitching pennies. They had even fought to a standstill once in sixth grade in their grammar school classroom wars.

Don handed Diego the money and bowed. As Diego unfolded the money and began to count it, Don's crew couldn't help but enjoy the look of amazement on his face. Diego realized too late he had played into Don's hand.

"That little bankroll, as big bad-ass Diego call it, is exactly one thousand dollars. A gee, a gangster. So that mean that Diego and his crew got to put up five thousand dollars. Five gees, cinco stacks. That is unless this stud been out here woofin' and he ain't got paper like that."

Knowing that his street credibility was on the line, Diego gave a halfhearted smirk and retreated to his homies. He instructed his main lackey, a tall, skinny kid with bad teeth by the name of Lonnie, to run to his Jeep and see how much was in the stash spot. In a few moments Lonnie returned with a handful of cash and a worried look on his face—there hadn't been as much cash as Diego thought. The rest of Diego's crew dipped in their pockets and pooled together the money they had on them. Altogether they came up with forty-three hundred in cash. Sajak, one of Diego's young dealers, offered a half-ounce of crack to the pot, and another, Monkeyhead, contributed a .357 Python revolver to make up the difference. Motioning to Don, Diego walked to the center of the basketball court.

"You think you slick," Diego grumbled when Don was in earshot.

Don retorted, "Nall, you think I'm slick."

"Fuck all of that shit. We got forty-three hundred, a half onion, and a heater. Is it a bet?"

"Hell yeah, but we choose who gone hold the loot." Don scanned the crowd and spotted an attractive teenage girl who looked innocent enough.

He turned back to Diego. "You see shorty over there in the jogging suit? We gone let baby girl hold this down."

Diego gave the girl a once-over. Nothing seemed amiss so he acquiesced.

Both boys sidled up to the girl, who coolly watched their approach.

Don asked, "Excuse me baby girl, what's yo name?"

"Juanita," she replied.

"Juanita, we need you to do us a favor if you ain't too busy right now. We want you to hold the pot for us while we play this game. You only give this shit to the winner. Is that cool with you?"

"Yeah, okay, but what do I get out of this?" she asked coyly.

"Well, you get to be my special guest of honor at the victory celebration," Don answered, winking as he handed her the winnings. "And after that, we will see what will be, baby girl."

Both teams stepped onto the court and took practice

shots on opposite ends of the court. After warming up they met in the middle of the court.

Diego announced, "We shooting from the top of the key to see who get first ball. Do or die on y'all, Don-Don."

Keno, Don's team's best long-distance shooter, easily sank the shot securing their team the first ball.

From the first pass, Don and his team controlled the tempo of the game. They had been playing basketball together since grade school. They knew each other's talents and strengths and covered one another's weaknesses. Diego and his team were the exact opposite. Every one of them thought they were better than they really were—everyone wanted to be the superstar. They consistently turned the ball over, hogged it, and forced up wild shots.

The beginning of the game was a little rough, but that was to be expected in a game for such high stakes. Don and his crew didn't back down; they were used to playing under intense pressure. Big Man snatched rebounds greedily at both ends of the court. Carlos and Keno shot jump shots from every angle on the court. Don was an astonishingly quick defender. He managed to steal the ball repeatedly from Diego and Lonnie and he blocked three of Monkey-head's shots. Dre had a dazzling array of layups in his repertoire and he drove to the hole with intensity.

Diego's team was out-classed, out-rebounded, out-shot, and out-passed. Before they knew it, it was game point with Don's team leading 32–14.

Dante inbounded the ball to Dre. Dre pushed the ball up

the court and passed it to Don. Don fed Keno at the top of the key. Keno was wide open and his teammates expected him to let fly one of his high, arching jump shots. Don and Carlos set two consecutive picks to free up Big Man from his defender. At the top of the key Keno flicked up a long, high lob. Big Man ran, leapt into the air, caught the basketball in midair, and slammed it through the basketball rim. Before letting go of the rim he smacked the metal backboard.

Holding his head in his hands Diego sat down in the middle of the court. He watched enviously as Don and his boys ran over to Juanita to claim their winnings. Don kissed the girl quickly on the mouth—she didn't protest. Laughing and congratulating themselves, Don's crew exited the fence surrounding the court. Don stopped and called Juanita over to the fence. He slid a fifty-dollar bill through the links of the fence.

"Shorty, that invitation still stands. We'll be over Semo's house on Eberhart. It won't be hard to find. You'll hear the music and smell the weed before you find the house."

Juanita thanked him and assured him that she would be there. As she turned and walked away, Don watched her plump behind for a few moments before running to catch up with his friends.

Keno said, "Man, that's a fine young bitch. If you get her naked don't forget to share. You know what they say. It ain't no fun if the homies can't have none."

Don teased, "They wadn't talking about you niggas that be burning all the time."

Big Man joked, "That nigga keep crabs like pets."

They all laughed.

Don thought about the pistol tucked into his waistband. "Come on y'all, let's put some pep in our steps, I got this heater on me."

2

AFTER A QUICK SHOPPING SPREE THEY ALL SHOWERED
and dressed in their new, stiff clothes which, combined with
a trip to the barbershop, had them looking like different
people. Even Semo was sporting a fresh fade and a new pair
of Jordans. After all, they were partying in his house.

Semo's house was the usual party spot. Semo's father,
a long-distance truck driver and his only parent since his
mother had died from lupus five years ago, didn't come
home for weeks at a time and he always phoned first. He
knew that Semo partied hard, and since he was a bit of a
hellraiser himself, he didn't mind, as long as they didn't tear
the house down. His phone calls to tell his son that he was
on the way home were really an early-warning system to
give Semo time to clean up any mess and clear out any

houseguests. Partying and getting high were at the top of the list of things that Semo loved to do, especially if everything was free. Don gave him the important role of playing host and that was fine with him. His only duties were rolling the blunts, keeping the drinks flowing, and making sure that no freeloaders got in the spot. He loved rolling the blunts; it gave him autonomy over the weed and the chance to cuff a few blunts, which he did at every opportunity.

The party was going full blast by the time Juanita made her entrance. Don was so high that at first he didn't recognize her. He was smoking a blunt and nodding his head to the music blasting from the stereo. When he spotted her and realized who she was, he choked on the smoke in his lungs. She was looking good enough to eat in a miniskirt, tie-up Roman sandals, and a halter top. Her pixie hairdo perfectly framed her tan, thin face. Her large doe eyes were enhanced by thick eyelashes. Her full, pouting lips were coated with shimmering lip gloss. The halter top she was wearing displayed her blemish-free midriff. She had the legs of a long-distance runner and her round butt hiked her miniskirt up dangerously high.

Don did a double take that would have made the Three Stooges proud. Pulled to her as if he was hypnotized, he grabbed her hand and gave her a hug.

"What's up, baby girl!" Don yelled into her ear over the music.

"Nothing, what's up with you?" Juanita shouted.

"I'm tight. You want something to drink?"

"Huh?"

"I said you want something to drink!" he repeated.

"I'm straight, but it's too loud in here. Let's go outside or something!"

"I got a better idea!" Don hollered.

"Huh?"

"Follow me!"

Don grabbed her hand and led her through the party-goers up to the second floor. They walked down a short hallway, and then he ushered her through a door and closed it behind them. Semo's father's bedroom was strictly off-limits to ordinary partygoers, but not to Don-Don. He motioned for her to have a seat beside him on the bed.

"Damn, girl, you looking fine as hell in that outfit there," he said. "I bet you ain't even got no panties on or you got on one of them thongs. You got on a thong?"

"Yep," she replied. "A black silk one, too."

"Ohwee," Don whistled. "I loves me a girl in a thong. I bet you look sexy as hell in that boy, too. Can I see it?"

Juanita laughed. "Un-unh. I don't even know you like that to let you be seeing my thong. How do I know you ain't a raperman or something?"

Don was taken aback, but only slightly. "If you thought I was a raperman, why you come up here with me? If I was a raperman do you think I would be asking you could I see your thong? Hell nall, I'd be ripping off yo skirt and shit."

"For you not to be a raperman, you sure know a lot about how to rape somebody," she said slyly.

For a second Don was confused, then he realized she was putting him on. "Get yo ass outta here. Girl, you had me going. Wassup though? Can I check you out in that thong?" he persisted as he leaned closer and sniffed her neck. Taking a chance he licked the tan skin right above her shoulder.

Juanita giggled. "Boy, don't do that. My neck is my motherfucking spot. You'll fuck around and have me off in here in my thong for real doing that shit there."

Inspired, Don began kissing and licking her neck. As she leaned back a little and let him, he decided to try his luck and rest his hand on her chest. When she didn't resist he slid his hand under her halter top. She wasn't wearing a bra. Happily he toyed with her taut young buds and listened to her breathing begin to grow ragged. After playing with her nipples and sucking on her neck for five minutes, Don decided to go for the gold. He slid his hand from under her top and let it rest on her smooth tan thighs. He started at the hemline of her miniskirt and attempted to work his way under it.

"No," Juanita moaned as she clamped her legs together.

Not wanting to break the mood, Don obeyed her wishes. He didn't push any farther, but he didn't move his hand off her thighs. Instead he redoubled his efforts around her neck, running his tongue in and out of her ear. Her body trembled as he worked his magic and when he leaned on her to push her back on the bed again he met no protest. Again throwing caution to the wind, he slid her top off. Hungrily he began to devour her breasts. She moaned and rubbed her legs together but didn't stop him. Don tried again to get his hand between her thighs. This time she sat upright and pushed him off her.

Don begged, "Come on girl, don't do that. You got my dick hard as hell. I know that pussy of yours is wet. Come on baby, let me have some of that. You already know I'll take care of you. You see how I hit you earlier."

She said, "Look, nigga, you can cut that baby, baby, please baby, baby routine. I ain't the one. You need to save that shit for one of them dumb bitches downstairs. So what, you gave me a fifty when we was over at the courts, that's old news. The only thing that's gone get you in these panties is some of that good weed with some crack sprinkled on it and a few more of them dollars."

At her proposition Don sat up quickly, so quick that he almost made himself sick. He had to pause until the room stopped spinning. Once his equilibrium was reasonably centered he snapped.

"Bitch, what the fuck did you just say? I know you ain't no motherfucking crackhead! All of them fine-ass bitches downstairs and I end up with a fuckin' clucker! How a fine-ass girl like you end up fucking with yams?"

Juanita proceeded to strip away her miniskirt and halter. Her firm breasts jutted and her smooth thighs flashed dangerously in the low light. Jiggling delightfully in the lace thong, her butt was a sight to behold.

Unaware of his actions, Don licked his lips.

Well aware that she had his undivided attention, Juanita

asked, "Do this look like the body of a clucker? Do I look like a crackhead to you? Motherfucka, I don't think so. Nigga, I ain't smoking the pipe, the whistle, the hooter, or whatever y'all call it. I just like to crush down a rock or two and sprinkle it on my weed every now and then. It ain't like you smoking the pipe. You can get that good feeling without being strung out like them motherfucking hypes. Now if that's too much for a lil' boy, then I'll go find me a man that can handle it. I thought you was on top of things, Mr. Don-Don, but you in here acting like you ain't up on the real shit."

With a look of disdain, Juanita grabbed her clothes and began to dress. Don put his hand on her arm before she could step into her miniskirt. He couldn't pass up this opportunity. He came to a quick conclusion. He had heard people talk about smoking premos, caviar joints, or sprinkles, but he had never tried it before. Even if he didn't like the high it gave him, it was well worth a little discomfort to get in her panties. He would try the shit with her once, then try to fuck her brains out. When he was through he would tell her to beat it.

With his hand on her arm, he said, "Hold it now girl, I was just tripping. I thought you was talking about smoking the hooter. A nigga ain't fuckin' with that. Slow down though, shorty. Imma grab some yay and we gone kick it."

Don got up off the bed and walked over to the bedroom door and opened it to holler for Dre. The music was beating so hard downstairs that he knew there was no way that anyone could hear him. He had given up on shouting and was headed for the staircase when Dre came out of the bathroom to his left, zipping up his pants. When Dre saw Don he put his arm around his friend's shoulder and started to talk, but Don cut him off abruptly.

"Dre, shut the fuck up, I ain't got time to rap. Where is that coke that I told you to hold on to? You still got it in your pocket?"

Dre nodded.

"Give it to me. I want to put it up just in case the law raid the party or something."

Dre handed him the half-ounce. Don turned and walked quickly back to the bedroom before Dre had a chance to start running his mouth.

When Juanita saw the half-ounce of crack in Don's hand she smiled and picked up her purse. She began removing various articles associated with drug abuse from her bootleg Coach bag—a spoon, a small mirror, and some rolling papers. She instructed Don to place a piece of crack on the small makeup mirror. Using the heel of the spoon she smashed the crack rock and spread it around on the small mirror. Don produced a bag of weed, which she seized from his hand. After pouring it out on the nightstand she removed the few stems and seeds. She instructed Don to stick two sheets of Tops cigarette papers together and put some weed on them. Using a playing card she scooped up some of the fluffy, powdered crack and sprinkled it over the weed in the unrolled joint until there was almost no green showing.

She rolled the joint, licked the glue strip, and smoothed out the finished product. There was a lit cigarette in the ashtray. She took it and held it to the tip of the joint. The sides of the joint blackened instantly from the burning crack. She exhaled the pungent smoke and took another toke. She handed the joint to Don and laughed at his look of confusion when he tried to hit it and it went out.

"No, silly," she giggled, "you gotta hold the cigarette to it to keep it lit."

He followed her example. His first hit of the crack joint left him with an indescribable feeling. If he had to describe it he would have said that it felt like he orgasmed ten times at once. His second hit rendered the same feeling only to a lesser degree. Admittedly he was a little scared at first, but now his inhibitions went out the window. He was beginning to enjoy himself so much that Juanita had to remind him to pass the joint.

Two joints later Don was in a frenzy from the mixture of drugs in his system. Putting the pent-up energy to good use he and Juanita had sex for hours before Don drifted off to sleep. He woke up early in the afternoon to the odor of premos. Rolling over, he discovered Juanita perched on the edge of the bed halfway through a big, fat premo. She offered him the joint and cigarette. His first impulse was to decline, but he reached for them anyway. He finished the remainder of the joint while she rolled two more.

DON AND JUANITA HAD BEEN IN SEMO'S FATHER'S BED-
room for close to thirty-six hours. If it was left up to Juanita
they wouldn't leave until all of the crack was gone. As Don
sat up in the bed, Juanita stirred, but didn't wake. He pulled
the sheet off her to expose her beautiful body. He traced
her tan curves with his hand. Using one strong hand he
grasped her ass, with the other hand he spread her thighs.
She obliged him by spreading her legs even farther.

Don shucked his pants and boxers and dove between her
legs. He began to suck and bite on her nipples while pumping up and down like a piston.

Juanita groaned from his penetrating strokes. Thrashing
her head back and forth she wrapped her legs around his
back and locked her ankles. Using her strong legs to support

herself she lifted her ass from the bed and began to grind a counterstroke.

Her moans and pelvic movements spurred Don into a frenzy. Climbing the steps of passion he reached the top, then plummeted headlong into the depths of climax. After she unlocked her ankles Don rolled off her and collapsed on the far side of the bed.

While the sexual encounter seemed to have drained Don, it had rejuvenated Juanita. Leaping from the bed she stretched and bounced off in the direction of the bathroom. When she returned from the bathroom she picked up the premo that Don had in his mouth when he first mounted her. Following procedure she lit a cigarette and held it to the tip of the laced joint. In record time she was through smoking the first premo and rolling another. She paused to get a can of air freshener and light some incense. Grabbing a folding chair she pulled it over to the window and took a seat in front of the window, still naked. A breeze blew through the open window making the pale curtains flutter like butterfly wings.

She lit the second premo and looked at it. Lately it was taking more and more crack on her joints for her to experience that rip-roaring high of old. As she smoked the premo she turned to look at Don. He looked so powerful and sexy even in his sleep. She felt the area between her legs growing warm, then moist. The premo and the sight of Don's naked body was making her horny. He looked so peaceful that she didn't want to disturb him, but she was definitely aroused.

She moved over to the bed. Resting her head on his genitals she began to massage him until he began showing signs of life. Taking the head of his semi-erect member into her mouth she expertly sucked him to complete hardness.

Though he didn't want to wake up, Juanita's sucking mouth wouldn't allow him peace. She signaled to him to light a premo while she continued sucking, licking, and blowing. He followed her instructions. The combination of the premo and fellatio reminded him of lying on a beach with cool waves washing over his body. He felt alive. With each hit of the laced joint the feeling of her mouth on him grew more intense. He could feel an orgasm building. It seemed to start from the soles of his feet and the top of his skull at the same time. He could tell that he was about to blow his stack so he took a long, deep pull of the premo. He held the smoke until he choked and let go. Taking only enough time to put the remainder of the premo and the cigarette in the ashtray on the nightstand, Don curled up in the bed in fetal position, exhausted.

Juanita ran to the bathroom to clean up and when she returned, she glanced at Don, who didn't seem to have enough strength to pull the sheet over his naked body. She nudged him, but he didn't respond. He wanted some sleep.

Juanita had different plans though—she was tired of being cooped up. She grabbed the remote control and turned on the television. An advertisement for Six Flags Great America was on. She had always wanted to go, but there was never enough money in her household to go to the costly theme park. Don had the money though. It was time to see just how open his nose was for her. Talking him into smoking premos was easy, so it should be a small matter to get him to take her to an amusement park.

Rubbing his sweaty back she started in on him. "Don-Don, wake up baby. C'mon, boo. I'm sick of being cooped up in this room. It feel like I'm on house arrest or something. Get up. I want to go to Great America."

"Damn, Juanita, it's too damn early in the morning for this bullshit," he whined. "Shit, we done been up all damn night and shit. I'm finta sleep, shit."

"Fuck that. Wrong answer. I want to go today. You think that all you gone do is lay up in this motherfuckin' room and fuck me. Shit, my pussy is sore. I want to have some fun. If you won't take me, I'm sure that one of your friends will."

She got up from the bed and began to dress.

He watched her out of the corner of his bloodshot eyes. The desire for sleep tempted him to let her go, then jealousy took over. He realized that he would hate to see her with one of his friends. Swinging his long legs off the bed he grabbed his boxers and pulled them on.

"Awight, awight girl. Sit yo motherfuckin' ass down somewhere. I'll go holla at my niggas and see if they want to go."

He pulled on his pants and shoes and left the room. Downstairs everyone seemed to be there from two nights ago. It was early so he wasn't surprised that everyone was still asleep. There were liquor and beer bottles everywhere, pizza and chicken boxes on the floors and tables, and the ashtrays were overflowing. Sleeping bodies covered every couch, seat, and almost every inch of the carpeted first floor of the house. On the coffee table a partially nude girl slept using what appeared to be her missing clothing for a pillow.

"I can't wait to hear the story behind this one," he mused as he viewed her naked body.

Stepping over several of his friends he continued to the kitchen. As he pushed open the swinging doors he grimaced at the sound of squeaking hinges. In the kitchen he glanced at the wall clock. It was almost seven a.m. Stifling a yawn, he opened the refrigerator in search of something to eat. The entire contents consisted of beer in various forms—forties, cans, and sixteen-ounce bottles of beer—not even a cold cut was present. Several large pizza boxes were on the counter-top. He went through them and discovered two slices of pepperoni pizza. After warming them up in the microwave, he wolfed them down with a cold bottle of Budweiser.

Now that he had succeeded in killing his hunger pangs it was time to awaken his friends. As he exited the kitchen he realized that it would be easier to wake up Semo and Dre and give them the responsibility of arranging the trip. First he would have to find them—they could be anywhere in the house.

Semo's house was larger than the average ghetto dwelling. It had four bedrooms and three bathrooms, plus a fully furnished basement. Semo was the youngest of three children. His older sisters had long since left the nest, one for a high-paying consulting job in New York, the other to become a baby machine for a Caucasian dentist in Atlanta. Though his father rarely came home, he never once forgot to pay the mortgage, the bills, and buy food for Semo. Semo's allowance was a hundred dollars a week, which he managed to squander on weed, beer, and gambling.

Don found Semo sleeping facedown between two girls. "Semo. Semo. Wake up, nigga," Don whispered from the doorway. "Semo, get up, nigga, I need you to stand on this business."

His friend stirred, but only to turn to the side and bury his face into the back of one of the girls. Walking into the bedroom Don stood by the foot of the bed and called him again. When Semo still didn't respond, he grabbed his foot and shook him harshly. His friend rolled over and sat up. With the back of his hand he wiped saliva from the corner of his mouth. Bringing his eyes into focus he finally acknowledged Don's presence.

"Damn, Don, what is it?" he rasped.

"Time fo you to get yo ass up, nigga. Damn, you look fucked up in the morning. All ugly and shit."

"Fuck you, nigga. Hand me my squares," he said as he scooted to the foot of the bed. His movements woke up the other girl, who sat up. She didn't move to pull the sheet up over her bared boyish chest. Instead she looked Don up and down. Disinterested, she lay back down. Semo accepted the proffered Newports from Don. His friend raised his eyebrow at him and nodded toward the two women.

With a gravelly voice Semo said, "Nigga, that shit come from fucking with that white liquor. You know gin make 'em sin. That shit have the bitches horny as hell. Personally I don't like it, but it turns them into some super freaks."

"I see," Don said. "I was thinking, nigga. We need to go somewhere. Somewhere like Great America. Shit, we got the cheese. Can you put it together?"

"I'm on it," Semo said. "Now get the fuck out of my room."

At Great America, Don, Juanita, and the group went on all of the major attractions and tasted exotic foods. Don pitched quarters at one of the game booths and won Juanita a gigantic stuffed gorilla. Feeling like little kids, they got their faces painted and their names airbrushed onto their T-shirts. Everyone met at closing time and they boarded the bus for home. The trip home was decidedly different than the previous trip—everyone was exhausted. There was no excited chattering, only the snoring of teenagers. When they reached the city the bus driver woke them up and dropped them off.

As the tired group trudged toward Semo's house they began to come back to life. Big Man suggested they throw a barbecue. Looking to Don as their leader they waited for him to organize the troops. Don delegated responsibilities to each of his field marshals. They bought a quarter pound of weed from Momma Taylor's son, a wise teenager with dreadlocks known simply as Bohead Taylor. Keno and some of the girls went to buy chicken wings, hot dogs, and ground beef for burgers. Semo fired up the grill and Big Man hauled the stereo speakers into the backyard.

By one a.m. the barbecue was going full blast. The smell of good weed filled the air. Drinks flowed. Paper plates were filled with food, emptied, then filled again. Just as the merriment was reaching its peak, Diego and his crew strutted through the gate. A whisper went through the crowd and everyone stopped to stare at the gatecrashers. Expecting trouble, Semo slipped into the house. He ran upstairs and grabbed his father's double-barrel shotgun from the closet. He snuck down the stairs and crept into the back bedroom overlooking the backyard. From the window he leveled both barrels at Diego's head. He waited with his finger on the trigger for Don to confront Diego.

In the backyard, Don handed his plate of food to Juanita and hefted himself from the lawn chair. He pushed his way through the crowd to get to Diego. As he passed Keno, his friend slipped him the .357. He stuck it in the waistband of his pants, not bothering to cover it with his shirt. When Don came face-to-face with Diego, he scanned his face for any sign of animosity. Unable to detect any malevolent vibes from Diego, he stuck his hand out. Diego looked at it first, then grasped the outstretched hand.

"Diego, what's up, fool? What brings you down this way? You came to party and bullshit with us?"

"Nall man, I came to try and win some of my scratch back. That is if you niggas ain't spent it all up."

Don asked suspiciously, "What you mean, homie? You must have been up there at Harper Court doing some practicing and shit. Now y'all want a rematch. I thought you crack dealers was smarter than that. I know you niggas ain't throwing rocks at the penitentiary just to give us y'all money."

Begrudgingly, Diego offered a laugh, but Don could tell that he didn't really find his remark amusing.

Diego said, "Nall, we ain't on that. I got to admit that you niggas can play some motherfuckin' ball. But what y'all know about these here?" Pulling his hand from his pocket, Diego displayed a clean, new pair of white dice. He shook them for emphasis.

Don laughed. "Fool, you ain't said shit. Me, Semo, and Carlos the best dice shooters around this motherfucka!"

"Well, like I said, if you niggas still got some of my money left we can go do this shit. Just to make this shit interesting and to keep the petty motherfuckas out of the game, let's say that we start off shooting dubs."

"Twenty dollars, nigga. Shit, I thought you was gone say fifties or something. We can go gamble in the basement. No interruptions. Just follow me."

In the basement Don was joined by his friends. Pulling out wads of bills, all the boys got down on their haunches. Big Man held the shotgun while Don gave the .357 back to

Keno for added security. There was something about the presence of pistols that kept arguing to a minimum. Diego and his right-hand man Lonnie knelt alongside Don. They cast the die to see who would roll first; Lonnie was the lucky man. He peeled a twenty off of his bankroll and tossed it on the floor. Fading him for the twenty Carlos matched his bet. With a nonexistent shake, Lonnie slick-rolled the dice into the middle of the circle. Carlos grabbed one of the die before it could stop spinning.

Looking at Lonnie he sneered, "Nigga, what choo doing? I thought this was a friendly game. Fuck you trying to lay them down for?"

"Nigga, catch what you don't like! Point seen, money lost! You know the game! If yo ass is scared, nigga, then don't fade me!"

"You better calm yo ass down," Carlos retorted. "You ain't even got to trip. You want to lay 'em down, do yo thing, nigga. I got something fo yo ass, boy. Don't say shit when I bust my shot out. You gone wish we wadn't shooting no slick shots."

Carlos threw the die on the floor and Lonnie scooped it up. He set the dice in his hand and without so much as a small shake he slid the dice out into the circle. Both dice spun for a few seconds. The first die stopped, landing on six. The second die bumped off of Semo's shoe and landed on six also. Boxcars. With a stupid look on his face, Lonnie paid Carlos twenty dollars for crapping out. He paid to back the dice and shot again. This time he caught eight as his point.

There was a flurry of movement as everyone in the game rushed to bet for or against Lonnie. Confidently, Diego bet Dre, Carlos, and Don that Lonnie could hit a six-eight. Slick-rolling the dice again Lonnie promptly rolled an eleven. The losers bet again. The money had barely changed hands before Lonnie threw a seven to crap out.

Scooping up their money, Don and Carlos laughed in Lonnie's face.

Carlos joked, "This nigga done got so slick that he done slicked hisself out."

Don said, "You ain't lying, Carlos. For my money he can keep shooting that bullshit ass shot. I love pigeons like this."

Angrily, Lonnie kicked the dice to Carlos. He asked, "Is you niggas gone shoot the dips or run y'all motherfuckin' mouths? Carlos, it's yo damn shot, big mouth. I'll fade you for whatever."

For the next seven hours the game went pretty much against Diego and his crew. It was almost nine a.m. the next day before Diego decided that he had lost enough money and quit. With his tail between his legs, and thirty-five hundred dollars in the rear, he left Semo's basement.

Too tired to celebrate, Don and his friends crashed on the couches and beds in the basement. He didn't wake until eleven o'clock that night. He staggered upstairs to find Juanita. She wasn't in the bedroom. He searched the entire house, but she was nowhere to be found. He went back to Semo's father's bedroom and sat on the edge of the bed smoking a cigarette. Deciding to smoke a premo, he went to the closet to get the Baggie of crack. Reaching onto the shelf, instead of a plastic bag, he pulled down seven joints. Amazed, he dragged a chair over to the closet and stood on it to get a better look on the shelf. Nothing.

Feelings of betrayal washed over him as he realized Juanita had stolen the rest of the crack. They had been in the basement so long that he didn't have any idea of the time she might have left. "Fuck it," he said aloud. There was nothing that he could do. Using his cigarette he held it to the tip of a premo and laid back on the bed.

"WANDA, OPEN THE DOOR! IT'S ME, JUANITA. WANDA, GET yo ass up girl, we finta party!"

A sleepy voice spoke from behind the thick wood of the housing development door. "Juanita, do you know what time it is! I ain't got no money and if yo ass is in trouble you can turn yo ass right back on around. I got enough problems!"

"Wanda, bitch, open this motherfuckin' door 'for I kick this piece of shit off the hinges!" Juanita shouted while kicking the door to let her sleepy friend know she was serious.

"Hold on, bitch, you better stop kicking on my goddamn door before you wake up my damn kids with yo stupid ass! If you wake 'em, yo ass gone be the one that put them back to sleep! I just finally got all they asses to fucking go to sleep and you come over here making all this gotdamn noise!"

Using one hand to wipe the crust from the corner of her mouth, Wanda ran the other through her nappy hair. She hadn't been expecting company, but that didn't make a difference. She would have looked the same if she was. Anyway, what difference did it make? Juanita had seen her looking much worse than this. As she unlocked the door she wondered what Juanita wanted at this time of night. When she opened the door an early summer night breeze pushed its way into the room, kicking the stale air out of an open window. Juanita rushed into the room as soon as the door was opened. She almost bowled Wanda over as she came through the door. She pushed Wanda out of the way as she slammed and locked the door. From Juanita's wide-open eyes and paranoid movements, Wanda could tell the younger girl was high off of crack.

"Bitch, don't come up in here on that tweaking shit," Wanda said.

"Fuck you, Wanda, ain't nobody tweaking."

"Yeah you is, you tweaking like a motherfucka. Must have been some good-ass shit, too, 'cause you tweak city."

"Whatever," Juanita said as she looked around the urine-scented room. She took a seat on a reasonably clean cushion of the sagging couch. Inwardly she shuddered. She hated Wanda's nasty little apartment. If this had been daytime, babies—Wanda's or her trifling girlfriends'—would be everywhere, shitty diapers and spilled Kool-Aid on the floor, and soap operas, Judge Mathis, or Jerry Springer on the tele vision. Wanda was a lazy bitch and almost never tended to her dirty, ill-mannered children. She was glad they were asleep. The little bastards were nosy and mannish. The oldest boy at six years old was already a pervert, a trait which his stepfather Raoul, Wanda's boyfriend, encouraged. The boy made it his business to expose himself to Juanita whenever possible. His mother would just laugh and say that he was going to be ho-ish like his father. Once when Juanita had passed out on the couch she had awakened to find the little boy pulling her panties down. She was outraged and found it hard not to kick the little fucker in his gapped front teeth. Just the thought of that embarrassing moment made her shiver. Raoul had sat across from her leering all the while. Only the fear of her brothers restrained him. If Wanda wasn't Juanita's favorite brother's baby's mama, Juanita wouldn't fuck with her. Even when she did come over to see her nephew, he was usually asleep, shitty, or sick. All Wanda did was argue with Raoul, usually over the last sip of beer. Both of them were so petty that they deserved one another.

"Bitch, you still ain't told me why the fuck you woke me up," Wanda complained, rubbing her eyes as she pulled a cigarette from the box on the three-legged coffee table and lit it off the stove a few steps away in the kitchen. Wanda's eyes fell on the coffee table and she thought about how two years ago she had bought it along with the living-room set from the money her sister gave her when she let her use two of her kids on her income taxes. Now one of the legs was missing, broken during one of her numerous parties. Telephone books kept the scarred wood surface from falling down.

"I woke yo ugly ass up for this," Juanita said, pulling Don's crack from her purse.

The sight of the drugs woke Wanda all the way up as it made her choke on the harsh smoke in her lungs. There were no traces of sleep in her voice when she whispered, "Damn girl, who you done robbed?"

With a sly smile Juanita replied, "Girl, get the fuck outta here. I ain't robbed nobody. My new man gave me this shit. Girl, I got a vic. This nigga is so sweet. I ain't got to do shit but lay on my back, or suck on that nigga dick and he give me anything I want. I heard that there was niggas out there sweet as him but I wouldn't have believed it to be true until I met him. That nigga will do anything for this pussy and some of this head. I came over here to share some of this good shit with you. You know you my girl and shit."

Their conversation was interrupted by Raoul's sudden appearance; he smelled drugs like a police dog. He stood half asleep in the doorway of Wanda's bedroom in a dingy pair of boxer shorts and a T-shirt. Scanning Juanita's face he knew without her even saying a word that she had drugs. He walked past the two girls, snagged a cigarette, and went into the kitchen to light it off the stove. He returned to the minuscule living room and sat on the tattered and taped fake leather settee.

"Fuck!" Raoul muttered as one of the springs poking through the material scratched the back of his scrawny leg.

Juanita knew what was on Raoul's mind. He was so smug that she was tempted to get up and walk out the door. *That would fix his funky ass,* she thought. Conjuring a picture of Raoul chasing her down the street with his shit-scarred boxers flapping in the wind almost made her laugh out loud. *Enough bullshitting,* she thought, *I might as well get this leeching motherfucka high too. Ain't no way I'm finta leave out of here now, ain't no telling what Don'll do if I bump into him tonight.*

"Wanda, girl, close yo damn mouth and get me a mirror."

Looking at Wanda's face she almost laughed at the puppy-dog look on it. Answering her unspoken question, she said, "Imma lay out enough shit for all us to get high. Bitch, you know I ain't one of yo petty-ass check-day friends that just get you high right before you get yo aid check."

Relieved that Raoul hadn't ruined her chance to get high, Wanda went into the kitchen to retrieve her utensils from the cabinet over the sink. She pulled down a chipped mirror, an arsenal of cigarette lighters that had been rigged to produce a high flame, pieces of wire hangers, and a razor blade. Last, but definitely not least, her crackpipe. To her it was a thing of beauty. It was a delicate masterpiece with a graceful stem like a swan's neck. The bloated middle was adorned with butterflies in different stages of flight. Under the bowl the glass swirled into a pig's tail curl. It hypnotized her to light a rock in the bowl and watch the smoke wind its way through the fluted glass, always finding its way into her mouth. To Wanda it was her most precious possession. Even Raoul knew better than to touch it without her consent.

Returning to the living room with the paraphernalia, Wanda placed everything on the coffee table in front of Juanita. She took a seat as she watched her young friend dump some of the crack from the sandwich bag onto the mirror. All the while she caressed her pipe like it was a magic lamp and she was summoning a genie. Meanwhile, in order to maintain some semblance of self-control, Raoul began fidgeting with the cheap stereo sitting on two milk crates in the corner. The soulful sounds of smooth R&B filled the room. The music helped to ease the couple's tension as they waited for Juanita to ration out the crack.

Looking up from the tedious task of breaking the crack down with the dull razor blade, she wiped her forehead with the back of her hand. "Damn, Wanda, it's hot in this motherfucka. Why don't you bring the fan in here and put it in one of these windows."

Carefully, Wanda sat her pipe on the coffee table and crept into her children's bedroom to get the fan. She brought it into the living room and handed it to Raoul. Quickly he set it in the window and plugged it in. Juanita dug in her purse for the weed and Tops papers. She found the weed easily—she had stolen two dubs sacks from Don along with the crack. Tops, however, were a different story. She turned her purse inside out, but still no sheets.

"Damn!" she said aloud.

"What, what?" Wanda and Raoul chorused.

"I ain't got no fucking Tops," she replied disgustedly. "This is some bullshit. I left my motherfucking sheets at that nigga's crib."

This is perfect, Wanda thought. She decided to take advantage of the situation and use her influence over Juanita to introduce her to the pleasures of smoking crack on the pipe. It sickened Wanda to sit and watch the young girl waste perfectly good crack on weed and cigarettes. To a pipe smoker, premos were just a messy, smelly, time-consuming, round-about way of getting high. She had never dared complain to Juanita in the past because it was usually Juanita's crack, but she knew from watching her recently that the premos weren't getting her as high as she wanted to be. She was consuming damn near a dime bag of crack on every joint; it was time to stop bullshitting and graduate to the pipe. The same way that an older girlfriend of her mother's had turned her out, Wanda would return the favor and turn out Juanita. All she had to do was get Raoul out of the way for a few minutes and the deed would be done. She couldn't risk having him around when she was doing something as delicate as turning a new smoker out. Knowing Raoul, he would say some stupid shit and any spell she could weave with words would be broken. If she could convince Raoul's greedy ass to leave the house, it was a Chicago cinch that she could get Juanita to try the pipe.

Turning to Raoul, Wanda winked and said, "Raoul,

baby. Why don't you take that five dollars off the dresser in there and run to the store? Go get a four-pack of St. Ides and a book of Tops."

Raoul didn't catch her wink. He exploded, "Bitch, is you crazy? I ain't finta miss out on all this good yam, ho! Greedy-ass, pipe-head bitch, you just want to be by yo'self with Juanita so you can tell her not to let me get high! I'm sick of yo bullshit! Bitch . . ." His tirade tapered off as he caught Wanda's rapidly winking eye. Sensing that Wanda was up to something, Raoul left the living room, all the while mumbling under his breath. In their bedroom he picked up a pair of khaki shorts and slipped into them. He snatched the five dollars off the sagging dresser and headed for the front door. His house shoes barely made a noise as he descended the concrete stairs and headed for the store.

Going over to the door after his exit, Wanda slid the dead bolt lock home. She turned and looked at Juanita. With a syrupy sweet voice she asked, "Nita girl, while that petty-ass nigga gone to get you some Tops, why don't you let me throw one of them boulders on the whistle?"

Juanita complied. "Gone head, girl. You know I ain't got no problem wit you. It's that punk motherfucka Raoul. I hate his ass. Shit, you might as well have stayed with my damn brother if you needed a nigga to disrespect you. You need to cut his fake ass loose, Wanda. All he do is sit up and wait on you to get yo aid check and them crazy checks you get for them damn kids. That's a good-for-nothing-ass nigga, plus he low down as hell. That nigga would fuck a snake if somebody hold the head for him. Thirsty-ass nigga need to get him some business."

"You ain't never lied," Wanda agreed as she picked a choice rock from the plate and deposited it in the bowl of her pipe. "But I can't lie and act like he ain't the only man that tried to be here for me and them kids. All them other niggas will pump a bitch belly full, but when it come time to take care of the baby he be gone with the wind."

She flicked one of the rigged cigarette lighters and waved the flame back and forth over the bowl before sucking it in. She pulled the dirty, gray smoke into her lungs and exhaled after a few seconds. Moaning like she was experiencing an orgasm, Wanda exaggerated the effects of the hit. She pretended to let the pipe almost slip from her hand.

Her voice barely a whisper, she squeaked, "Girl, grab this pipe for me. Just hold it until I stop shaking."

Juanita rushed to Wanda's side and grabbed the pipe from her hand.

"Girl, what's wrong with yo ass? You bet not OD on me. I ain't finta be blowing in yo asshole or whatever you got to do to bring a motherfucka back from a OD."

Wanda waved her hand and clutched the neckline of her ragged nightgown. "I'm alright, girl. It's just that sometimes, when you get a good hit of yay without all that comeback, soda, and B-12 shit on it, it make you come on yo'self. Yo panties be wet, but the shit is worth it."

While she fanned herself, Wanda watched Juanita. She could tell by the way the girl was staring at the pipe in fascination it was now or never. Catching Juanita completely off guard, she asked, "Want me to hold the torch for you?"

They locked eyes for a few seconds, but to Wanda it seemed like an eternity. Thinking that she had overplayed her hand, Wanda was prepared to make light of the situation. The last thing she wanted to do was make Juanita think she was forcing her to hit the pipe. Inside she hoped that Juanita didn't get upset, take the crack, and leave. She allowed herself to breathe again when she heard Juanita say, "I know how to hold the torch—I ain't handicapped. Shit, I done watched you do it enough."

Before she got a chance to change her mind, Wanda snatched a piece of crack from the mirror and dropped it in the bowl for Juanita. She handed Juanita a torch and sat back.

As Juanita put the pipe stem to her lips a small voice within her cried out to deny herself this first real hit of crack. Ignoring the voice, she flicked the lighter and waved the flame across the pipe bowl. In a trance she watched the smoke curl through the pipe and then into her.

By the time Raoul returned from the store there was no need for Tops. Juanita had found a new friend.

5

DON'S NEW HABIT WAS INCREASING AT A MONSTROUS rate. Since Juanita had made off with his small supply of crack, he had secretly begun shopping with Diego's people. He hated to admit it, but he missed Juanita. He found himself thinking about her even when he was surrounded by other girls. He knew he missed their wild, drug-inspired sex sessions, but he also missed the fact that when she was around she shared the secret of his drug use with him, something he wouldn't tell even his closest friends.

The money he and his crew had won in the dice game from Diego and Lonnie allowed the party to continue for a few more days, but the constant celebration had decreased their funds at an alarming rate. Don had managed to cuff close to a thousand dollars for himself. His friends had no idea that he'd taken the money, but the paranoid mind frame the crack joints kept him in made him think that they were on to him and beginning to mistrust him. They were sitting back drinking beer and trying to figure out where all the money had gone when Don stormed out of Semo's house leaving his friends totally shocked.

When he opened the back door of his mother's house, Rhonda was in the kitchen making a sandwich. His older sister put down the piece of bread in her hand when he brushed past her. She started to initiate an argument with him, but one look at the expression on his face and she decided that it would be better to leave him alone. For the first time in her life she felt like she didn't know her younger brother. Somehow he managed to appear much older than his seventeen years. His boyish face was gone, replaced by a man's face—hardened and lined. His eyes seemed to hold a strange, hungry look.

Don bound up the stairs to his room.

Rhonda found herself sighing in relief as he went upstairs and wished that he would return to wherever he had been for two weeks.

Later that night his mother came into his bedroom, hollering at the top of her lungs.

"Donald Haskill! Wake your ass up right this minute! Where the hell have you been for two weeks? Boy, you ain't grown! You must be losing yo gotdamn mind! Who the hell do you think you are walking in here after you been gone for two damn weeks?"

Don awoke at the sound of his mother's irate voice and stared at her for a minute trying to focus his weary eyes. "C'mon Ma, you acting like you didn't know where I was at. I called Rhonda and told her to tell you where I was. You hollering and I got a headache."

"This is my damn house! I can holler around here as long as I want to! You don't pay no damn bills around here! Boy, I know for sure that you have done lost your damn mind! Who do you think you talking to? I ain't one of your little hoodrats! I wish your father was here to set your ass straight! You wouldn't be doing this stuff if your father was alive! I swear, I work too hard to have to put up with this bullshit!"

Deciding that he had his fill of his mother's yelling, Don turned toward the wall with his back to her. That only made her yell louder.

"What the hell is wrong with you, boy? Your ass is gone end up in jail running them streets like you ain't got the sense God gave a billy goat! I didn't raise you like this! I don't go to work and school so you can have a place to lay your head when you're tired of running the streets! You think it's a joke out there! Yeah, it's big fun! It always is until somebody blow your gotdamn head off or you get yo ass into some trouble that you can't get out of! I see young boys like you all the time! Think they so smart and they know it all! We stuff little boys like you into body bags every day! Donald Haskill, I am talking to you! Do you hear me?"

He pulled the cover over his head. "Yeah, I hear you, Ma. Everybody in the neighborhood can hear you. You picked a fine time to come up in here with all that hollering. You finally managed to remember that you got two kids and now you want to act like a mother. You don't be acting like a mother when you over yo boyfriend's house. You don't come home, so why should I?"

Baffled, Hazel Haskill stood for a second looking at her son's form under his covers. She let out a disgusted sigh as she quietly said, "I don't believe you just said that. I guess that I was wrong thinking that my almost-grown children could understand that for the first time in a long time, I'm happy. You are not about to make me feel guilty for living my life. I've always taken care of my children and you're not going to make me feel like I haven't. What I don't deserve to have someone who cares about me and that I enjoy spending time with?"

"I don't care, Ma. It's your life. Like you said, we too old for you to be worrying about. I won't do it no more. Now can I go back to sleep?"

"You know what, Donald, forget it," she said. Knowing that she was wasting her breath, she stormed out of his room and slammed the door.

Don knew from experience that his mother's bark was a thousand times worse than her bite. She had yelled at him millions of times, but she never hit him or threatened to put him out. It was so rare that he saw his mother, he hated that she seemed to be yelling whenever he did. Underneath the covers he drifted off into a fitful sleep.

It was storming outside when he awoke the next after noon. With his bedroom window wide open he sat and watched the jagged lightning flash across the sea-water–hued sky. The heavy rain pelting against the trees, cars, houses, and concrete made him depressed. After checking to make sure no one was home, he returned to his room and watched the thunderstorm as he smoked premos.

Later in the evening the storm passed and he ventured out. His small supply of drugs was dwindling and he needed to pick up a few bags of crack. He still had a couple of nickel bags of weed, but without crack he just didn't want to smoke it. As he dressed, looking out the window, the dark streets of the ghetto looked inviting.

He headed out the door with the pool hall in his mind, but his feet steered him toward Harper Court. Along his journey he spotted a familiar figure standing at the bus stop. He slowed his walk to make sure that he wasn't hallucinating or mistaken. It was Juanita.

Quietly he snuck up on her. She never felt his presence until he had backhanded her in the mouth. He complemented the slap with a left jab to the ribs that buckled her knees. He rocketed a right hand to her jaw that lifted her off her feet to finish her off. With a whoosh she landed on her butt, hard. He prepared to stomp her.

"Bitch, where my shit at?" he snarled.

Juanita lay on the ground holding her jaw with one hand and her ribs with the other.

"Damn, Don, you ain't have to hit me like that. I ain't do shit."

The sight of her on the ground with her miniskirt hiked up exposing her scar-free, caramel legs aroused him. Don realized that he really wasn't all that angry about the crack she had stolen. He was just going through the motions. Grudgingly he admitted to himself that he really missed her—her company, her soft body, her expertise with her mouth. Extending his hand, he helped Juanita to her feet.

Inches from her face, he threatened, "First of all, bitch, if you ever steal anything from me again, Imma stomp yo fuckin' guts out. Imma shoot you in yo fuckin' thieving-ass hands. Second, now you my motherfuckin' woman so where the fuck is you going?"

Cowering, she answered, "I was finta go to the Westside and try to find my brothers so I could get some money to get something to eat. I'm hungry as hell."

"Well, bitch, you ain't going to the Westside no more, you going with me. I'll feed you as soon as I pick up this package from them niggas at Harper Court. C'mon."

Don started walking. Happy to be let off the hook Juanita fell right into step—plus she knew what he was going to Harper Court to get. They walked along silently until they reached the gate to enter the park. Diego wasn't around, but his workers peddled his wares, regardless of weather, time, or police. Don swung the rusty gate open. He approached one of the workers and purchased an eightball. Elated that his cop was successful, they went to Don's house.

At home, Rhonda was preoccupied in her bedroom with studying and talking on the telephone, so she didn't see the couple walk past her room. Once in his room, Don went through the ritual of placing a towel at the bottom of his door. Juanita sat on Don's bed and looked around. It was a typical teenage boy's room. Posters of basketball players and rappers hung on the wall and a few small trophies were displayed on the top of Don's dresser. Clothes were tossed on the floor.

As Don prepared to smash down a piece of the eightball to make crack powder, he asked, "Bitch, what was you thinking when you ran off with my shit? I couldn't even believe that you peeled me like that. What—you wadn't having a good enough time?"

"It was cool," she pouted. "When y'all got to gambling you forgot all about me like I didn't mean shit to you. That hurt my feelings. At first I thought you was really digging me, but the minute Diego and those fools showed up you didn't pay me any more attention. That made me jealous and mad. That's why I took yo stuff so you wouldn't never forget me again."

"Shit, you tripping on that dice game, Diego and them goofies had big paper on them and we was trying to separate them from it. I'm sorry that it took so long, but when the gamble is good you got to stick with it. Now gone stick a few Tops for me and help me break down this weed."

In silence they removed the stems and seeds from the weed and each of them set up a joint to be rolled. Don sprinkled his with crack rather thoroughly, but if his was a snow-fall, Juanita's was a blizzard.

"Damn, girl, I can't even see the weed on that boy with all that coke on it," Don commented as he sealed his premo.

"It's just that Diego and them shit be a little weak," Juanita said bashfully. "You got to really lace these mother-fuckas to get high."

"Whatever," he said as he waved his lighter back and forth on his joint to dry the rolling papers and fuse the mari-juana and crack together. After smoking his premo and en-gaging in another marathon sex session with Juanita, Don fell fast asleep.

However, Juanita was wide awake. She waited until she was sure that Don was sound asleep and called his name softly several times. When he didn't respond she was satis-fied that he wouldn't awaken anytime soon. She retrieved her purse from the dresser. She opened it and removed a glass crackpipe and a cheap cigarette lighter. Wanda had shown her how to take the metal part off the lighter and use the small lever in the back to turn the gas up to pro-duce a makeshift torch. Her crackpipe wasn't as elegant as Wanda's, but it got the job done. First she inspected it for cracks in the glass and then she made sure that the screen was still in place. She pinched a rock from the pile of crack on the saucer under the bed and dropped it in the pipe bowl. Flicking the lighter, she held the orange flame to the crack and with her lips on the stem pulled the white-hot smoke into her mouth. The rock sizzled on the pipe screen and melted.

Don caught her completely off guard. He snapped, "Bitch, what the fuck do you think you doing!"

Juanita was so scared she almost dropped her pipe. She was busted—there was no denying it. It was too late to hide her equipment. Now if she could just get out of this one without getting her ass beat.

She crawled on the bed with Don and pressed her naked breasts against his chest. With her free hand she gripped him between his legs. With tugs and jerks she began to arouse him. He felt his nature rising, but tried to ignore it and pursue his line of questioning.

"Bitch, I know you ain't smoking the hooter in my momma's house! Let go of my swipe, you hear me talking to you!"

"I'm sorry Don-Don, I wasn't trying to disrespect yo mama's crib. It's just that after that good fucking you just gave me I wanted a bump off the whistle, you know. If you want me to leave, then I'll go."

She accentuated every word with flutters on his member. She could tell that he didn't want her to go. Since Wanda had turned her on now it was time to pass on her knowledge.

She cooed, "Don-Don baby, I'm sorry, boo. It's just that I was looking out for you. We be wasting all that good-ass crack on them pussy-ass premos. All we smoking is paper.

That shit don't even get me high no more. And if you think it feel good when I suck yo dick when you smoking a 'mo, wait till you try it smoking the pipe."

From the curious expression on his face, Juanita knew Don was buying her line of bullshit. A little more prodding and he would be eating out of her hand.

Meekly, Don asked, "Girl, how you know that shit ain't gone fuck a nigga around? I mean smoking 'mos is one thing. To tell you the truth they ain't get me anywhere near as high as they used to. I'm cool with premos. That way you smoking weed and crack, but with the pipe all you smoking is crack. The hooter ain't shit to fuck around with. I heard that shit can kill a motherfucka. I ain't finta be no hype neither."

"Don, I know a down-ass nigga like you don't believe everything you hear. A big, bad nigga scared of the little ole pipe." She laughed scornfully. "Everybody is doing this shit. You can't even tell because everybody don't turn into no clucker. That only be those weak-minded motherfuckas that can't handle their drugs. Them and old people. Young people like me and you can't get addicted like that. Plus them people's lives already be fucked up. Then they start smoking and everybody want to blame it on the crack, but how you start off is how you finish. If you was fucked up before you started smoking then you gone be doubly fucked up when you is smoking. But look at people like me and you. This shit can't fuck us up 'cause we already straight. Plus with premos all we doing is smoking the paper pipe. Smoking crack is smoking crack, I don't care how you do it. Plus you don't have that crazy ass noid feeling that weed give you. You better get with it. This shit is going on. It makes you feel like a super motherfucka. Try it. I guarantee that you ain't gone never find nothing that make you feel as good as this."

Juanita's words, and her grinding and fondling of him, had him confused. Before he knew it Don had the glass stem between his lips taking his first blast. Juanita doubled his pleasure by giving him a simultaneous blow job. To him, it felt like his entire nervous system was being sucked into her mouth. Somehow he managed to synchronize his next hit with his ejaculation. He wanted to scream for her to stop, but he didn't dare. Dropping the lighter, he sank back onto the pillows. He never saw Juanita's sly smile as she headed for the bathroom to rinse out her mouth.

TWO-AND-A-HALF WEEKS HAD PASSED SINCE DON'S first hit of the crackpipe. He had spent every last cent of the money he had stolen from his friends. It had taken the connivance of his girlfriend and the space of a little over a month and a half to change him from a friendly, outgoing youth into a paranoid recluse. Juanita was his constant companion. He ventured outside the safe confines of his home only for crack or cigarettes.

Dark circles appeared under his eyes from lack of sleep; his weight dropped off by the pounds. His diet consisted of candy bars, Cheetos, and chicken wings. Don's once unblemished face was now pockmarked with pimples and blackheads.

For a time his friends still tried to kick it with him, but they found him distant. They were unaware that his growing crack habit was responsible for his aloofness. He began to borrow money from them and never repaid it. Dre, his best friend since third grade, knew that Don was going through a thang, but he didn't suspect that his troubles stemmed from drug abuse. Not one to abandon a friend, Dre tried for a while to tolerate Don's moodiness, but even he began to fade out of the picture.

Rhonda had no idea of what was going on with her little brother. She blamed Juanita for all of her brother's recent changes. All she knew was that before Juanita started coming around her brother seemed normal. Rhonda hated the hold Juanita seemed to have over Don—she couldn't stand the girl. It was exasperating to see that young tramp leading her brother around by the nose.

One Saturday morning when Juanita walked to the store to buy a couple of loose cigarettes, Rhonda decided to try and talk to her brother about his girlfriend. She knocked on his door.

"Who that?" Don asked as he duffed the pipe he was cleaning under his pillow.

"It's Rhonda," she said sweetly. "I want to holler at you for a minute."

"What you want?"

"Boy, let me in this damn room."

"Hold on," Don said as his eyes swept the room to make

sure there wasn't any incriminating paraphernalia laying around. Content that he could stand a light inspection, he walked over to the door and lifted the latch. "Come in, girl."

Rhonda entered the room, noticing a strange burnt odor, but she didn't know what it was. She looked over at her brother. He had returned to his bed and flopped across it. "You need to let some air in this damn room, boy. It stink in here. I hope that ain't yo feet smelling like mildewed cardboard."

Don raised his middle finger. "I know you ain't bother me just to tell me that my room stank. You worry about your room and I'll worry about mine. What you want?"

"Look boy, I just came up here to see what's up with my little brother."

"What you mean what's up with me? Shit."

"Something's up. You don't kick it with yo buddies no more. No basketball. A couple of weeks ago you couldn't be paid to stay in the house, now it seem like you never leave. You used to attempt to go to school, but a letter came from the school saying that you haven't attended school this semester. I ain't even showed it to Mama yet."

"She don't care. If it ain't got nothing to do with them fucking cops, a schoolbook, or her faggot-ass man, she don't want to know nothing about it."

"Mama do care. It's just that for the first time in a long time she got a chance to be happy. She ain't got to be here nursemaiding us. We grown. Well I am anyway, you just think you grown. Laying up with that little hood booger."

"That's what this about. Juanita. You just don't like her. Well, you ain't got to like her. She's my woman. What yo lonely ass need to do is get you a man so you can stop worrying about what I'm doing and who I'm doing it with. Sound like you jelly of her."

Don's comment blew Rhonda's mind. "I know you don't think I'm jealous of that slut. You have got to be kidding me. Jealous of what? She ain't got shit. Not a pot to piss in or a window to throw it out of. Boy, you are really bullshitting yourself if you think I'm jealous of that homeless-ass tramp."

"Yeah, well why you all up in here talking shit about her," Don snarled.

Rhonda had to catch her breath before she said any more. She hadn't come up here to argue with her brother. "Look, Don-Don. I just came up here to check on you. I don't know what's going on with you, but I don't like it. You done lost all yo weight and your face is looking bad. You ain't had yo hair cut and there's a crazy odor always coming from yo room. You can talk to me 'bout anything. I'm your big sister and I love you."

For a moment, Don looked like he was about to cry. In all honesty he wanted to tell his sister everything; that he might be in over his head, but the thought of being without Juanita and without crack stopped him.

"Yeah that's right," he said. "You my sister, not my mama or my daddy so keep yo nose out my personal business. Now is there anything else?"

Dismissing his disrespectful tone, Rhonda said, "Okay Don, but like I said I'm your big sister and if I can help you in any way I will."

"Whatever," Don said to the room's closing door as Rhonda left. He pulled his pipe from under the pillow and resumed trying to scrape some residue from under the lip. The stuff that Rhonda was talking about wasn't shit. He was broke right now and didn't know where he was going to get his next hit.

Rhonda passed Juanita on the steps as she was going downstairs. Rhonda wanted to hit Juanita in the mouth for whatever she had done to her little brother, but instead she headed for her bedroom.

When Juanita entered the room, Don was racking his brains for a way to come up with a nice piece of cash. He decided to try and get his friends to play another basketball game. With no scratch of their own they would have to rely on Dre to steal some of his brother's cash. To gain their help, he knew he would have to apologize for his recent behavior. That was something that he wasn't looking forward to. Since Juanita was dropping hints that if she couldn't get high here she would go somewhere else, he knew that he didn't have much of a choice.

Don got up and began to slip into his hooping gear.

"Where you going, baby?" Juanita asked.

"I'll be back. Imma try to hustle us up a nice rack of cash so we can chill for a few more days. I think I got a line on some loot, so hold fast and I'll be back."

"What am I sposed to do while you gone? It's boring here."

Quickly growing irritated with her whining, Don snapped, "I don't know what the fuck you sposed to do. Watch some motherfucking TV or something. I said that I'll be back. Now stop fucking with me."

Don left her on the bed looking salty as he dipped out of the house. The pool hall was his first stop. If his friends weren't there it would still be easy to pick up their scent. In his mind he was spending their winnings. Maybe he could talk Diego into putting up another half-ounce of crack— that would be an acceptable bonus. Reaching the game room he walked inside. Nobody from his clique was present. That was a minor setback, but one he could deal with. He scanned the room and located a likely candidate that might have information pertaining to his friends' whereabouts.

"A homie, you seen Semo, Big Man, or Dre and nem?"

The cornrow-wearing youth's eyes never left the video game he was playing as he said, "Yeah, they was up in here awhile but they left a coupla, few minutes ago."

"Did they say where they was going?"

"They had mentioned Momma Taylor's house, but that was all I heard."

Don was already out the door. He knew if they were following their old routine they would probably be at Semo's house by now.

Using the alleys and gangways he reached Semo's house in a matter of minutes. As he came around the garage behind the house he could hear his friends' voices. For the first time in weeks he realized just how much he missed his friends. He realized that he had replaced their constant companionship with Juanita and crack cocaine. They had grown up together, braved the dog streets of Chicago's South Side together. They had faced bullies together, stole together, fought together and one another. It brought tears to his eyes thinking about all the things they had been through together. Composing himself, he put his hand on the rusty gate. With a shove he opened it. Standing perfectly still he watched the boys for a moment. They were so engrossed in one of their petty sports arguments that they didn't notice him.

Keno looked up and saw him standing there. He signaled to the others that they had a guest. Everyone stopped talking at once and looked at Don.

He felt a little self-conscious under their stares at first, but he knew it was now or never. He walked over and sat on a lawn chair. Under their collective scrutiny he felt anything but at ease. He tried to play it cool. With hooded eyes he stared at his sneakers waiting for one of them to make the first move. It didn't take long.

"What you want, nigga?" Big Man drawled.

"Yeah, nigga, what brings you around?" Semo added.

Don said, "I just wanted to see you studs. I mean damn, we is homies and shit."

"That's not how you been playing it since you hooked up with yo new broad," Semo countered.

Apologetically, Don offered, "Man, I'm sorry 'bout all that shit. Ain't no thang, you know. It was just I made a mistake is all. Pretty little bitch had my head all fucked, yo. I can't even front. I'm cool now, though. My fault if I seemed like I flipped on y'all niggas."

"Yeah, nigga, you was in love like a motherfucka," Carlos said. "Now get you a beer and hit some of this blunt, nigga. We yo niggas, we ain't tripping on that little shit. We glad you back, we sick of hearing Dre bitch-ass whining 'bout missing you."

Carlos held the lit blunt out to Don.

"No thanks, kid. Since we back down and shit, let's make some loot so we can throw a big-ass party. I'm talking 'bout some off-the-hook shit. Dre, run to the crib and grab about three stacks. Shit, hopefully we can get Diego to at least go for three-to-one odds. Shid, we gone stomp them niggas. I been working on my game and shit . . ."

Don was talking so fast he never noticed the looks of disappointment on his friends' faces.

Semo interrupted. "Slow down, nigga. Is that what you came over here for? Dude, you outta pocket. We really missed kicking it with you, dog, but I see all you missed is having us help you make some scratch."

"Nall, Semo, you got me all wrong, I didn't mean it like that. I was just thinking on the way over here that it would be fun to kick Diego and them ass for some of that easy money so we could throw a party."

"You mean so you could buy you some crack don't you?" Carlos interjected. "Nigga, we played them studs last Sunday for five gees. We won of course. And while we was at the court Diego noticed that you wadn't playing and mentioned just how good a customer you done became. Nigga, we knew something was wrong wit yo ass."

"Man, I don't know what the fuck you talkin' 'bout. I know y'all don't believe that funky-ass half-breed. I been copping from him, but it was so I can get my swerve on. I been hustling so I can help out at the crib and shit with the bills."

"See, I told y'all he wadn't fucking with that shit," Dre said, wanting to believe that Don was straight. "He been copping pieces trying to get his pockets right."

"Dre, shut yo ass up," Carlos said. "Look at this nigga. Do he look like he been hustling? This nigga is clucking. Look at all the weight he done lost and shit. His face skinny as hell. Tell me he ain't starting to look like a baby crack-head."

Don looked around at his friends. Dre was the only one that seemed to hope that the rumors weren't true. He decided to try and bullshit his way past them. "Come on y'all, this is Don-Don. Do y'all think I'm a fucking clucker? I done lost weight 'cause I be stressing and I don't be eating right. Think about who it is y'all talking to."

"We know who we talking to, a motherfucking crackhead," Big Man said slowly. "I got enough of them in my family for me to know exactly what they look like from start to finish. Nigga, you know that all my uncles is on that shit, so I know."

Don began to grow angry. He shouted, "Y'all sposed to be my niggas, but y'all gone let some motherfucka tell y'all some foul shit about me! That shit ain't cool. I ain't done shit to you niggas. How y'all gone turn y'all back on me?"

"Nigga, you turned yo back on us," Big Man said with his usual country twang. "We been through a lot of shit together. If you had came to us with the real we could have helped you with whatever, nigga. How you gone play us?"

Semo said, "Man, fuck this crackhead-ass nigga! He better get the fuck out of my yard, before I whoop his motherfucking ass!"

Don was dumbfounded. "Semo, who the fuck you think you talking to, nigga? Yo pussy ass. Nigga, all of a sudden you tough. I'd still beat the dog shit out of you, bitch-ass nigga!"

Keno spoke up for the first time. He threatened, "No you won't, hype. 'Cause if you put yo hands on Semo we gone stump yo ears together in this motherfucka."

Looking in Keno's eyes, Don saw that the lanky teenager spoke the truth. They were prepared to beat him down. With a mask of scorn on his face he glanced at the others. He could tell that they echoed Dante's sentiment. Only Dre, his oldest friend, looked confused. In a last desperate attempt he tried to play on Dre's uncertainty.

"Dre, I know you ain't gone front on me like these niggas. Cut these fake-ass niggas loose and ride with yo man. Nigga, we been down since like eight years old. We don't need these punks. Scary-ass niggas. Come on Dre, let's be up."

Before he walked out of the gate Don paused to see if Dre would follow him. He locked gazes with Dre and knew his efforts were futile when the boy dropped his eyes to his shoes. At that moment he knew that he would miss Dre the most.

Giving Dre a way to save face, he relented. "It's cool, Dre. Don't even trip. I don't need none of y'all. You niggas turned y'all back on me, but I'll be alright. Fuck y'all."

Don slammed the rusty gate and savagely kicked an empty beer bottle as he stalked down the alley. As disgusted as he was at his friends' treachery he had no place to turn now. He knew that if he went home empty-handed, Juanita would be talking shit. He walked and cursed his bad luck, especially the misfortune of having Diego run his mouth off to his friends.

Damn, I could use a blast, he thought. *Then I could get my mind right.*

With nothing else better to do, Don did what so many other tortured Black men do every day—he stood on the nearest corner. He extracted a crumpled cigarette from his pocket and lit it. Gagging at the taste of the stale smoke, he spit a piece of tobacco out of his mouth. Deep in thought, he paid no attention to pedestrians. From the depths of his brain he recalled a small bit of information that could end his crack strike. If he remembered correctly, Diego gave credit to good customers. The interest on the credit was ridiculous, but that was beside the point. Paying back double wasn't so bad, especially when you could have a credit line of up to four hundred dollars. Snapping his fingers he put his feet in motion and headed for Harper Court.

Arms and legs pumping like pistons, Don ran like a world-class sprinter. By the time he reached the small neighborhood park he was out of breath and had to sit down on the curb for a moment. He didn't want to approach the crack dealers sweaty and looking like he was geeking for a hit. Coming off like a hype would destroy his chance for getting a piece on consignment. On the curb he rehearsed the lines he would use like a theatrical understudy. Using his T-shirt he wiped his forehead. He got a sip of water from the water fountain in the middle of the park. He spotted Diego. The drug dealer was doing his usual strutting in front of some young girls of suspect age.

"Yo, Diego, check it out," he called pleasantly, closing the distance between himself and the drug dealer.

Diego instantly recognized from Don's patronizing tone that he wanted a favor. He had been selling drugs long enough to know that when customers was short or didn't have any money they could be the nicest people on Earth. The closer Don came, Diego could see for sure that his old archrival was a fucking clucker. The sly smile that played upon his lips showed his pleasure at seeing Don like this. Now that Don was a crack monster he knew the boy wouldn't be challenging him anymore.

Diego asked, "What's up, Don-Don? How you living yo?"

"I'm tight, bruh. I just came to check you out. I done ran into a little snag with this scheme I'm running. My loot is low right now, so I was hoping that you could hit a nigga up wit a little something to hold me over until I get my paper in order. You know I'm good for it."

Diego had heard it all before. "Yeah, you good for it. You done spent a decent piece of paper wit a nigga. But I'm duty bound to let you know that all credit cost double. And even a cool fella like you got a deadline like everybody else or . . ."

"Yeah, Diego, I know all that shit. But you don't got to worry about that shit. Once my little scam come through I'll have some nice paper."

Nodding, Diego said, "Awight, Don. I hope you right, 'cause I don't want to have to come looking for you. What you trying to touch?"

Throwing caution to the wind, Don said, "Nothing huge, just a quarter. That should hold me until I touch this paper I've got coming to me."

Diego looked him up and down. "Run over there and tell Lonnie that I said to give you a quarter ounce."

"Thanks, bruh," Don said, hoping that he didn't sound too eager. He backed away to find Lonnie quickly in case Diego changed his mind.

The business transaction with Lonnie took only a few seconds. Don had to admit that they did have a smooth operation. It took only a nod from Diego and he had seven grams of crack in his hand. He ran all the way home with the quarter ounce stuffed in his pocket with his hand on it.

Bursting into the house, Don bound up the steps and crashed into his room. Juanita was lying in the bed. She appeared not to have moved an inch since his departure. He walked over to the bed and triumphantly dangled the quarter ounce over her head. She bolted upright and retrieved the saucer from under the bed. Razor blade in hand, she waited eagerly for him to dump the contents of the plastic bag on it.

"See, girl," he bragged, "I told you that I was gone cop. I ain't no shorty in this shit. If you stay with me and act like you got some sense, I'll keep both of us high."

Stroking his ego, she said, "You know I love you, baby. I wasn't worried 'cause I know that my man can handle his business. I knew that you wasn't coming back without some shit. To celebrate after I take me a hit Imma try to suck you dick to the bone."

Don took off his shirt and shorts. Chivalrously, he waited for Juanita to take a bump off the pipe so he could receive his reward.

7

A QUARTER OUNCE OF CRACK FOR SMOKING PURPOSES was considered to be a lot, but Don and Juanita consumed it in record time. Two days of continuous smoking and sex was all the time they needed.

Juanita was relentless. "Don, you need to do something. That little shit we had is gone. I need something else."

"I know," Don said as he scraped res from the pipe. "You think I don't know that shit, girl. Shit, the way you smoke we need about a ounce to hold us for a few days."

"I know you ain't talking the way you be sucking up the yams. I didn't see you holding back none."

She was right, they had both grown piggish when it came to smoking crack.

Juanita got up and tossed the television remote on the

bed. She stretched and put her hands on her hips. "I'm 'bout to get up out of here."

"What?"

"I'm 'bout to show at the crib," she said innocently. "I ain't been home in a coupla weeks."

"Who you live with?" Don asked. "You never did tell me about yo crib and you never act like you got to go there."

"I live with my drunk-ass momma and my four brothers when they ass out of jail. They don't care if I come to that motherfucka or not. Plus me and my momma stay into it. Whenever she get drunk, which is all the time, first she want to be all happy. Next she get to doing all that crying and bringing up the old days. Then she get straight-up mean and start talking shit."

"Okay, well, why you fixing to go there then?"

"I need to change clothes and see what's going on around the crib. I been cooped up in here for too long."

Don thought about it. He guessed that if he let her out of his sight she might not be coming back anytime soon. No crack was one thing, but no crack and no Juanita was unfathomable.

"Bitch, you better sit yo ass down somewhere. You ain't been worried about changing clothes or going to the crib. Now all of a sudden when the rest of the yayo gone, then you ready to hit the crib. That's bullshit. I know what yo ass trying to do. You done smoked up all my rocks and now that we ain't got shit, you ready to be out. You got to be crazy than a motherfucka if you think that you leaving up out of here. I'll kick yo head in. If you leave up outta here it's gone be in a ambulance."

"Well, what you gone do?" Juanita said as she bounced onto the edge of the bed and folded her arms. "I want a bump."

"Shut the fuck up so I can tell you what I'm gone do. A nigga can't even think or get a word in edgewise with you talking shit. Now look, I need you to call one of them jiffy cabs."

"For what?"

Don reared up and raised his hand. "I swear if I got to tell you to shut the fuck up again, I'm gone slap the shit outta you. Don't worry 'bout for what, bitch. Damn! You getting on my motherfucking nerves with all these questions. I said call a motherfucking jiffy cab. Now gone head. I gotta do something."

Don descended the stairs from his room to the second floor. He dipped into his mother's bedroom and began rambling through her dresser drawers. He found her old wedding ring, an antique brooch, and two gold chains. From the shelf in her closet he pilfered his mother's video camera. He fled his mother's room and pushed open his sister's bedroom door. From the top of her bookcase he took a 35-millimeter camera. He looked around for something else and found a thin gold chain on her dresser. He took everything downstairs and set it on the kitchen table. He slid into the living room and unhooked the VCR from the television. Back upstairs, he grabbed a pillowcase to stash the merch in.

Outside a car honked.

"That's the livery cab," Juanita called out.

"Come on, girl. You going with me."

"Where we going, Don?" she asked, eyeing the pillow-case.

Don rolled his eyes. "Bitch, you just don't learn. Stop asking so many questions and start waiting for instructions."

She followed him outside the house to the cab. As they slid into the backseat, Don said, "A mellow, take us to 47th Street to the pawnshop. She gone wait with you while I'm the spot so you don't think I'm trying to get ghost on you for yo fare."

On 47th Street, Don went into the pawnshop on the corner of Prairie. About ten minutes later he returned without the pillowcase and hopped in the backseat.

Juanita was excited. "How much they give you for that stuff, baby?"

"Don't worry about that," he said, but he was thinking, *not as much as I should have got.* "A homie, you know where Harper Court is? Over by Stony Island?"

"Yeah," the driver said. "You going that way?"

"That's right. Then take us back to where you got us from." He lowered his voice to Juanita. "Look, when we get to the park, I want you to run over there and grab us a eight-ball."

Juanita's lips instantly poked out at the word *eightball.* "That's all? We went through all this for a funky little ball?"

Don pulled out a couple of hundred dollars. "That ain't all we can afford. I got us enough for a piece, but we finta take it slow this time. When we through with that we gone get some more, but this time I want to make it last a little longer."

"Oh, okay," Juanita said as she snuggled up against Don's arm. "I knew you had more money, I just didn't know what you was trying to do."

8

THE DEADLINE FOR PAYING HIS DEBT TO DIEGO WAS swiftly approaching. Don didn't have four dollars, let alone four hundred. He knew that Diego and his cronies wouldn't be playing when they came to collect. The last thing in the world he needed was a pumpkin head. He had too much pride in his looks to be walking around with a swollen face. Things had changed. Don never thought he would see the day that he was prepared to duck Diego.

Back in the days when he was with his clique he had garnered respect from all the thugs, dealers, and bangers. Even the infamous Apostles had tried to recruit them, but they had decided that they didn't want anybody calling the shots for them so they declined the gang's offer. It had looked like it was going to get hairy for a moment; the Apostles weren't used to being denied. But since they didn't want anyone to be a part of them that didn't want to be there, the Apostles backed off.

These days, his clique was gone. The only thing he had left was Juanita's crack-feigning ass and his .357 Python. It was a heavy pistol, but it was well balanced. Its chrome frame glistened like molten silver when it was polished. True, it didn't have the stopping power of the .44, but when it spoke, people listened.

The more he thought about it, the pistol was the answer to his financial problems. Desperate times called for desperate measures. He would have loved to have the luxury of trying to talk someone out of their money, but nowadays con men didn't make very much in poor communities. Being a stick-up kid seemed like his last resort. The very words—*stick-up kid*—made the hairs on the back of his neck stand up. The stigma surrounding armed robbers was enough to deter all but the truly desperate. In the inner-city, people tolerated almost every kind of human animal that preyed on others except for the stick-up man. Drug dealers, flesh peddlers, thieves, and gangs were looked at as the norm, but armed robbers were despised. No matter whether they stole from hardworking people or other criminals, everyone hated them.

All of that was beside the point. Don needed money and he needed it now. In his heart he knew that without the backup of his friends, he didn't need to have an enemy as powerful as Diego. He would make getting Diego's money his main priority. Last, but certainly not least, he needed some scratch to get high.

As he dressed in dark clothes, more and more places he could rob popped into his head. He wasn't dumb enough to rob someone from the hood. Pickings would be better farther north or south. If he remembered correctly there was a steel mill around 79th Street over east by the lakefront. Across the street from the mill was a tavern where the workers stopped to grab a cold beer or whatever when they got off of work. The steel mill paid so well that most of the time the dirty, thirsty men would have pockets full of money to drink or gamble away before going home to their wives. They got paid every week so they always had money. He had gone there to gamble with steel-mill workers on several occasions. Most of the men had been easy pickings, but inclined to get violent when the young boys won too much of their hard-earned money. Today was Wednesday. The steel mill paid its workers on Tuesdays so Don knew the mill workers would be drinking and gambling for certain. Transportation wouldn't be a problem. The 27 South Deering bus would let him off about a half block from the joint. He would worry about the return trip when the time came.

As Don ducked into his sister's bedroom and relieved her of two bus tokens, he thought about her comment that things were coming up missing in the house of late. He was high at the time so he gave her some bullshit excuse. He wasn't sure whether she bought it or not, but he knew that she wouldn't turn him in to their mother.

Back in his own room he told Juanita, "I'm 'bout to raise up outta here. I got business to tend to."

For once she didn't start in with the questions. She had noticed that he was dressed all in black and he had his pistol with him. He left the house.

At the bus stop he had to wait only about five minutes for a bus. Once he was on the bus Don sat in the back and went over the plan in his mind. He got off the bus on 79th Street and walked to the bar.

Ben's Bar and Grill was strategically located across the street from the largest steel mill in Chicago. All a worker had to do was walk out of the mill's gate and cross about fifty feet of pavement to enter the popular watering hole. The patronage consisted of mill workers and prostitutes; there were always men willing to pay for pleasures of the flesh. On the corner of the same block sat the Lakefront Motel, a good place to rent a room by the hour to enjoy a quick roll in the sheets with a prostitute.

When he entered the smoky, dimly lit tavern, Don was disappointed to find it almost empty. Leaning against the cigarette machine he caught the attention of a tired-looking, bleached-blond hooker. Crooking his finger at her, Don signaled for her to come over. She flounced her hair, slid off the vinyl bar stool, and approached him. She tried to walk over to him sexily, but the hooker succeeded only in looking ridiculous. It was hard for him not to laugh as she drew nearer.

"Excuse me, baby, I ain't looking for no action right this minute, but I want to know if they still be gambling in the back room."

She pulled her gum halfway out of her mouth and twirled it on her finger, trying to look sexy. Again he was forced to suppress his laughter.

"No. Everybody got tired of Ben trying to house the dice. They started renting rooms at the Lakefront on the corner to gamble in. They don't even buy his beer and whiskey. They get it from the liquor store down the street and it's cheaper." She sucked her gum back in her mouth and licked her lips. "Is you sure that's all you want to do is gamble? I know a young stud like you could really make a girl feel good. I usually charge fifty, but for you I'll give you an around the world for half that." She caressed his face softly, and he found it hard not to recoil in displeasure. "Forget about that old dice game. You can put that sweet meat of yours anywhere you want." She used her other hand to grope at his crotch. "Yeah, you got a nice one. You could fill me up. I'm tired of these half-dead mill workers. They can't get it up at home or with a real woman like me. That's why they all want to play kinky games and shit. I know a young bull like you won't have them problems."

Don had to untangle himself from her hands as politely as possible. "That sounds real good, baby, but I'll have to take a rain check. Right now I need to get to that dice game and trim a few of those pigeons. When I come back with my pockets all nice and fat then me and you can slip off for a few hours. Shit, if you tell me what room they in we might just spend the night."

The hooker's eyes lit up as she calculated the money he would have to spend to retain her services for the night. If she fucked him to sleep, she just might be able to make it out of there with his whole bankroll. "The manager usually give them room 303. You don't even have to stop at the desk. Just walk on up. Tell them Constance sent you. And you better come back in here and get me when you win. If you do I'll make sure that you never forget me for the rest of your life."

"I will, boo," he promised, as he managed to escape her clutches with only one pinch on the buttocks.

Constance stood at the window of the tavern and watched him walk down the street. A steel-mill worker opened the bar's door and stepped inside. Like a parasite Constance attached herself to his arm and followed him over to the bar.

Once Don was out of sight of Ben's, he sat on a bus-stop bench and re-thought his plans. In a way he was glad that the dice game had moved from the bar to the motel room. That lessened the chance of some cop walking in on his robbery. Plus, Ben was an ornery old fool, meaning he more than likely had some heat behind the bar. He smiled, not believing his luck. All of his pigeons were cornered in a small motel room—it should be a cinch to get the drop on them.

He wasn't really worried about them being heavily armed; they usually carried only small case knives, but he wouldn't underestimate them.

More than anything he wished he could have a quick hit off the pipe to give himself a boost. Pulling a cigarette pack from his pocket he extracted a cigarette and half of a premo. Filled with nervous energy, he held the lit tip of the cigarette to the blackened tip of the caviar joint and inhaled deeply. The laced joint didn't even begin to compare with a blast from the whistle, but it did take the edge off of his nerves. He smoked it down until the roach burned the yellowed tips of his fingers. He smoked the remainder of the cigarette, tossed the butt into the gutter, and left the bench. A half block later he was in the lobby of the motel. The young woman behind the desk filing her nails never looked up once as he strode across the worn carpet of the lobby. With Constance's instructions in mind he took the steps two at a time to the third floor.

He passed two doors on the third floor before he came to the one with 303 emblazoned on it. Outside the door he could make out the voices of the men gambling inside. There was no mistaking the universal language of dice. Hoping he wouldn't have to shoot anybody for trying to be a hero, Don knocked on the door.

He heard someone say, "Shut the fuck up, it sound like somebody at the door!" The silence that ensued was his cue to knock again. This time a gruff voice asked, "Who is it?"

"It's Henry," he said trying to make his voice sound as grown up as possible, "I just came from Ben's and Constance told me I'd find the game here."

It didn't take any more than that. The door swung open and he stepped into the room. The gamblers paused for a moment to look him over then resumed their game. He could tell from their loud voices and boisterous behavior that they were all intoxicated. As he kneeled on the floor beside them, they didn't seem to notice that he never pulled out any money or attempted to join the game. Like a vulture waiting for a man to keel over in the desert, he watched the game until he was totally sure that they were all off guard. There seemed to be a decent amount of money in the game, so Don decided that it was now or never.

Standing up quickly, he snatched his pistol from under his shirt and held it to the head of the man closest to him. "Alright! You motherfuckas know what the fuck this is! Everybody get on the fucking floor! If I gots to say that shit again this motherfucka right here gone lose his memory!"

One of the gamblers, a brash, foolhardy fellow by the name of Conrad Stevens jumped to his feet and charged head-down like a ram at Don. Sidestepping the man's football charge, he smashed the butt of the heavy pistol on the base of the man's skull. The hard blow along with his obvious intoxication rendered Conrad immobile. His chance to be a hero thwarted, Conrad passed out in the middle of what was once a lively dice game. To add insult to injury

Don viciously stomped the man in the face. Sweat rolled down his face and a mad gleam was in his eyes.

"The next motherfucka that try some hero shit is gone be in a funeral home by tonight! Now who the fuck want to be in Gatlings? You can either go home broke or go home in a box! Now make me act a fool up in here!" Don kicked Conrad in the face again. "I came here to get money, not to hurt no motherfucka! Now if the rest of y'all can act like y'all got some sense, this shit can be over quick and everybody get to go home instead of to the funeral parlor!" He reached into his back pocket, pulled out a plastic shopping bag, and tossed it into the middle of the room. "I want the closest motherfucka, that's you in the blue shirt, to pick the fucking bag up and put yo fucking money in the bag."

The steel-mill worker, a big, burly guy, hurried forward. He was so terrified of the fierce youth with the huge, chrome revolver that he forgot to stand and moved forward on his knees. Don had to bite the inside of his bottom lip so he wouldn't crack a smile.

"Alright motherfucka, move back and pass the fucking bag! And hurry the fuck up!"

The men in the room complied quickly, dumping their money into the bag and passing it along. Don noticed that the few women in the room, obviously prostitutes, shunned the bag.

"Whoa, whoa, you motherfuckas pass that bag to them bitches too! I know these hoes got some paper—they been in here with all you big spenders! If I got to go in one of y'all funky pussies or strip-search one of yo hoes Imma wile out in this bitch!"

The threat of a strip search prompted the women to delve into their bras and panties and remove wads of bills, grumbling all the while. With his gun leveled at his hostage's navel, Don bent over and snatched the money out of Conrad's hand. By now the bag had returned to the man in the blue shirt. Don motioned with the pistol for the man to bring it over. Quickly, the man crossed the room on his knees. He dropped the bag at Don's feet and looked up at him. He was shaking.

"Get the fuck back over there! Now two of y'all pick this hero-ass stud up and take him in the bathroom! I want everybody to get asshole naked in this motherfucka and get in the bathroom!"

Grumbles erupted all over the room. Don raised his pistol and started randomly aiming it at his victims. "I didn't ask none of you niggas to comment! I don't remember taking no vote or shit! This ain't no fuckin' democracy! Shut the fuck up and get that shit off!"

Everyone in the room stripped noiselessly and began to crowd into the bathroom. Faced with the confines of the bathroom a few of them grew bold enough to complain again.

Don snapped, "I said this shit ain't up for discussion! Now shut the fuck up and get in there! I know it's tight! Get the fuck in the tub, stand on the sink, I don't give a shit, but you motherfuckas better get in there and hurry this shit up!"

When the last person was in, Don shut the door. He dragged a chair over to the door and propped it under the doorknob. The makeshift lock wouldn't hold them for long, but it would give him enough chance to escape. Peering into the bag, he knew he had hit the jackpot. It looked like he had more than enough to pay off Diego and to support his habit for a couple of weeks.

As he left the room Don blew a kiss in the direction of the bathroom. There was barely an audible click as he closed the door behind him. Bailing down the three flights of steps he only slowed down to cross the lobby, not wanting to attract any unwanted attention. Through the lobby's glass doors he spotted a cab pulling up to the red traffic light at the corner. He burst through the doors and sprinted to the cab. The dreadlocked cabdriver unlocked the rear door and Don climbed in with a wide grin on his face.

"Take me to Harper Court," he said.

DON DIDN'T WAIT FOR ALL THE MONEY TO RUN OUT BE-
fore he hit the streets this time. He still had a few hundred
left over from the hotel-room heist and he had an idea how
to use that to get more. He remembered once when he was
about fourteen, he, Dre, and Carlos had caught the bus over
to Jew-town to buy some shoes and they'd bumped into a
guy hustling three-card monte. The guy had taken them for
everything they had, but Don had paid close attention to the
game knowing he would use the knowledge one day. His
hands were quick so he began practicing a bit in his bedroom.

"Juanita, see if you can find the red queen."

She was fumbling around with the pipe, which seemed to

be a constant practice of hers these days. "I don't want to play no cards, Don. I'm trying to clean this whistle. On my last hit I could tell that the screens were clogged."

"Girl, put that shit down and check this out. I ain't playing cards. I'm finta show you the way we finta get us some money. Now get yo ass over here."

"Okay, okay. Show me."

"Now pay close attention, 'cause this shit is serious. If we don't do this shit right we could get fucked up."

"We?" Juanita asked. "What you mean by we?"

"Just what the fuck I said. You got to help on this one. I need a motherfucka that can work the crowd. Yo job is just to win. The pigeons watch you win and that's what gets them to bet they cash. The whole trick is that you got to act like you don't know me. And you got to play it up big when you win, but not too much."

"I don't know 'bout all that, Don. I ain't never done no shit like this before. How the hell Imma know what to do?"

"If you pay attention and shut the fuck up I'll show you what to do. Now check it."

Don's hands were a blur as he maneuvered the playing cards around facedown on his dresser top. "Pretend like you're a regular passenger on the train. Remember you don't know me."

"I got it, damn. How many times is you gone say that shit? I ain't slow."

"Girl, c'mon. What's up, baby girl, you feeling lucky

today? Ten will get you twenty, twenty will get you forty. Give it a play, this may be your lucky day."

"I don't gamble, mister."

"This ain't gambling, baby girl. Gambling is when you can lose. This here is a sure thing. I know somebody as pretty as you got some money. C'mon and double your money, sweet thing."

"Okay, man, but this bet not be no scam. I got twenty dollars to blow."

"That's good. Not too eager. Okay, take your pick, sweetheart. Now once you place your bet you got to watch my face. If I look to the left it's on the left. Straight at you then it's in the middle. To the right and it's on my right. This is important because I can't put it in the same place every time or watchers will get suspicious."

"What I'm sposed to do after I win?"

"Once other players get in then I want you to fade back instantly. Once I take off a decent piece of cash I'll signal you and that means get off the train on the next stop. I'll get off on the stop after you and link back up with you."

"That's a lot to remember, Don. When is we gone start doing this shit?"

"Tomorrow, so you better pay attention and get it right."

"Alright, alright."

"Alright, my ass. Let's go over it again."

They practiced for the rest of the evening and the next morning. By afternoon, Don was confident that they were ready to try the scam for real. They hopped the El train on 63rd Street heading downtown. Don brought out the makeshift cardboard table and the three playing cards. Juanita was just a microsecond off on her cues, but all in all she wasn't bad for her first time. By the time they reached the Loop, Don had fleeced several passengers of about 140 bucks. He gave Juanita the signal for the fadeaway and she got off the train. It was pretty crowded so he took a chance and got off with her.

"I told you this shit was gone be sweet," he said as they crossed over to the other side of the El station to go back the opposite way. "We ain't gone be greedy. Duff this money. We gone ride this boy back the other way and see what we make."

On the way home Don was in high spirits. They had cleared close to $250. Elated, he waved the money in the air. "We just made a couple hundred for taking a motherfucking train ride. I told you this shit was gone work. You did good too, girl. At first you was a little shaky, but in a couple of days you'll be a pro."

"In a couple of days? I thought we was just doing this shit today. I ain't know that you was talking 'bout doing this shit all the time."

"Girl, is you crazy? Look at the money we just made. I'm doing this shit every motherfuckin' day. I'm finta get my paper."

The next two days went about the same, but by the fourth day the daily commuters began to warn the unsuspecting riders against playing Don's rigged shell game. Their last few days out they made only enough to cover their traveling expenses, and after a close call with the transit authority police, Don decided to pack it in.

Disgusted, Don sat on the side of his bed with his shirt off and his pipe in his hand. "Damn, all these motherfuckers hating and shit. They just mad 'cause we been taking they damn money. Pigeons need to mind they own damn business. They done fucked up a nice little hustle with all that damn hating. It ain't like we was robbing no motherfuckers or shit. Shit, if you don't want to lose yo money then don't play. Do you want to find another train to get down on? I hate missing that Loop train though. That's where all the pigeons be. We ain't make no cash on no other train but that one. We finta leave this shit alone. What you think, baby?"

"It's cool with me," Juanita agreed readily. She was still thinking about a heavyset woman that drew her index finger across her throat at her. "What you want to do now though, baby? You know that we got to keep hustling."

Don was pensive. "I don't know. I was thinking about bouncing out to O'Hare airport. I heard some cats talking. They was saying that motherfuckers out there be sweet as hell. Out of town motherfuckers sightseeing and shit. Thinking they still at home in them small-ass towns. Heads be in the clouds and shit. The cats that was talking 'bout the shit was some cannons."

"Cannons?" Juanita repeated.

"Pickpockets, girl. Damn, where the fuck you been? Cannons is them studs that be beating motherfuckas for they wallets and purses and shit. Stealing vics checkbooks and writing bogus paper. Then they use the credit cards to buy merch, fill-up niggas at the gas station, all that shit. Them niggas be clean, too. Suits and dresses and shit. I know a little bit about dipping."

"What's dipping, baby?"

"Girl, you dumb as hell. Dipping is going in a nigga pocket. I think I know how to dip regular wallets and shit. I mean, how hard can that shit be? I ain't fucking with them checkbooks and shit, though. We gone catch the train out to the airport tomorrow and Imma see how sweet that shit really is."

It was his second day at the airport before Don had the nerve to pick someone's pocket. His clumsy attempt netted him three days in the county on a petty theft charge. He used an alias and was released on an I-bond.

At home, he had a long-overdue reunion with his crack-pipe. He was glad that he had taken a few moments to hide the cash and crack they had on hand before they left for O'Hare. He didn't believe that Juanita would steal from him again, but he decided against tempting her. Miraculously, Juanita showed up on his doorstep the second day after he was released. When he opened the door she jumped into his arms.

"Damn, baby, I missed you so much," she said, hugging his neck. "I damn near shitted on myself when them security guards grabbed you. I didn't know what to do."

Don detached her from his neck and held her at arm's length. "What the fuck you been doing while I was locked up?"

"I ain't been doing shit, baby," she replied. "You can ask yo sister. I been over here every day to see if you got out. I wanted to stay, but yo sister wouldn't let me in. Shit, what we gone do now, baby? The airport dead and I needs me a bump."

Don grabbed her hand, led her into the house, and up to his room. They spent the afternoon smoking crack and having wild sex. Afterward Don sat on the edge of the bed smoking a cigarette and thinking about his next move.

Three-card monte was out of the question and so was pickpocketing. He had about $812 saved and an eightball of crack. While he was locked up he thought about selling crack. It was a logical move. Lots of people loved to smoke crack—his neighborhood was full of cluckers. Why couldn't he cop a piece and slang a little himself? He had the money and the know-how, plus he could cop from the cats at Harper Court. He stubbed out his cigarette and lay back on the bed.

Even though he hadn't served a bag yet, Don had visions of getting rich. He could see himself driving expensive cars and dressing fly from head to toe. He knew that some of the ghettos' biggest dealers had started off from meager beginnings.

Don would find out there was only one problem with a crackhead selling crack: They smoked up most of the product before they could sell it.

He purchased a quarter ounce from Diego to start. Juanita helped him bag it up and Don hit the block with ten bags in his sock. He walked up and down the block for two hours before he finally landed the first customer. A short, schoolteacher-looking lady bought four dime bags from him. Feeling triumphant from his first sale he ran home to tell his girl the good news. He found her with the pipe to her lips preparing to take a blast.

With fear on her face she sat frozen, scared to put the torch to the pipe bowl. Her voice was shaking when she spoke. "Don, don't hit me, baby. I ain't steal nothing, boo. You said you wasn't gone hit me no more. Please don't start tripping."

Don closed the room door and stood looking at her. She looked a mess. Her hair was undone and standing all over her head. Her womanly curves had a lot less curve to them. As he stood there, he realized that he wasn't even angry. To keep her off balance, he said, "Bitch, I'm out there hustling and you up here smoking the shit. How much of the shit you done smoked?"

Carefully Juanita sat the pipe on the bed. "Just a couple of bags, Don. You was taking so long and wadn't nothing on TV, so I took me a few bumps." She braced herself for the punch she knew was coming.

Instead of hitting her, Don stripped off his T-shirt and picked up the pipe. Using the torch he took a long hit. "Bitch, what the fuck is you balling up like that for? I ain't finta hit you. I'm finta go back out, but I just wanted to take me couple of bumps first."

He pulled the remaining bags from his sock and opened one. He dumped it in the bowl and held the torch to it.

The first bag started a chain reaction. A day and a half later, they had smoked them all. Though he still had close to six hundred dollars and an eightball in the stash, Don decided against pursuing a career as a drug dealer.

While they smoked the eightball, the couple racked their brains for a way to make money—fast money.

"I got it, baby, I could hit the streets and turn a few tricks with some of these balling-ass niggas," Juanita suggested.

The next thing she knew she was picking herself up off the floor. She held her jaw where Don's slap had left a handprint.

"Did I ask you to sell pussy, bitch?" he snarled.

Juanita just shook her head and held her jaw.

"Bitch, I don't ever want to hear you say no shit like that ever again. As long as I'm your man ain't no woman of mine gone be hooking with these funky-ass niggas."

"I wasn't talking about the regular niggas, baby," she croaked out. "I was talking about hitting up some of these paper-getting dudes."

"Bitch, I wouldn't give a fuck If it was Oprah Winfrey wanted you to suck her pussy. I catch you turning tricks and you gone be eating dinner with a straw 'cause Imma break yo gotdamn jaw."

"Well, what you want me to do, boo?"

"Nothing right now. We ain't hurting too bad. I'll figure some shit out and let you know if I need you to do something."

Not wanting to see their bankroll disappear, Don hit the streets. He snatched a few purses, stuck up a few small dice games, and snatched a couple of gold chains—nothing very lucrative.

During the weeks that passed Don learned through the ghetto grapevine that his old clique was getting rich on the streets. Dre's brother Zack had put them in the game with a vengeance. The report was that Zack had fronted them ten grams of heroin apiece. The dope was real good, and they were able to put a five on it. Don knew that anytime you had some dope that could be cut five times it had to be a bomb. Zack taught them how to mix the potent synthetic narcotic with milk-sugar and how to set up a successful heroin peddling operation. In the couple of months since they'd fallen out, his ex-friends had their own cars, money, and jewelry. They were serving in the Wells. The Wells was a mile-long stretch of housing development units on the Low End of Chicago's South Side. When it came to drugs, the Wells was a gold mine.

After hearing the news, Don was salty. He knew that he

should have been right there beside his friends, getting rich. It was depressing, thinking about the money his friends were raking in, so he dismissed their good fortune from his thoughts. Right now he needed a new hustle—one that would bring in some gees. Sitting on his ass daydreaming wasn't paying shit, so he grabbed his pistol and left the house.

On his way to the pool hall he ran into Monkeyhead sitting at a stop sign in his bloodred two-door Chevy Caprice about to make a turn. The large boy was one of Diego's main flunkies. His name fit his face with its huge, purplish lips, wide, flat nose, and close-cropped kinky hair.

Don greeted the man-sized teenager. "Monkeyhead, what the deal, yo?"

"Nothing much, Don-Don," Monkeyhead said. "What's up with you?"

"I'm chilling, joe. I was finta go to Deon's. Where you headed?"

Monkeyhead wiped his dark face with the back of his hand. "Was on my way to Harper's Court. I just came from the rim shop. I was trying to buy some thirties and Vogues for my Chevy, but them studs want too much goddamn money. Cheapest I was looking at was about twenty-two hundred."

From the look on Monkeyhead's face, Don could tell that he really wanted those tires and rims. Thirties and Vogues seemed to be the rage with all the street dealers. Don knew that the boy could afford it, but who wanted to pay all that money? He had to admit that the shiny-spoked rims and Vogues with their gold stripe seemed to bring out the hidden beauty of a big-body automobile like the Chevy Caprice. It had never crossed Don's mind to steal and sell the expensive auto accessories. The average dealer in the market for rims and tires would jump at the chance to buy the stuff at street value—half of the retail price.

"Yeah, some clean-ass thirties with the gold caps and some meaty Vogues would look right on this boy," Don asked, testing the waters.

"I know that's shit."

"What if I can get you some shoes for yo Chevy at half the store price?"

The ape-faced boy smiled. He had always liked Don and still liked him even though he was a hype. His smile was one of doubt because he knew crackheads always made promises they never kept. Halfheartedly, Monkeyhead said, "Nigga, if you bring me some decent thirties I'll put the money in yo hand with no problem. Long as it ain't no slum shit. Or no Mexican-ass, gold-dipped shit. I want chrome with gold caps. None of them bald-ass Vogues neither."

A sly smile crossed Don's lips. "Alright, give me yo math. As soon as I get hold of what you was looking for I'll hit you. I hope you gone have that paper."

On a little notepad mounted on the dashboard Monkeyhead wrote his number and handed it to Don. Then he peeled off.

Don stood on the corner looking down at the scrap of

paper in his hand. *This shit is right on time,* he thought. Monkeyhead had opened up his eyes. The young dealers were always buying cars and decking them out. They almost always wanted rims, tires, and sound systems. That was right up his alley. He already knew how to steal cars.

He had stolen plenty of cars with his friends when he was younger to learn how to drive. Usually some unlucky working stiff's car, but that was the way things were around here. The only things he would need were a strong flathead screwdriver and a driver. The driver's job would be to take him out cruising for a vehicle to purloin. Finding a driver wouldn't prove too much of a task. He knew quite a few hypes who owned cars and would jump at the chance to make some easy money.

After purchasing a screwdriver, Don walked two blocks over to St. Lawrence. He was looking for a clucker that went by the name of Weed-Eyes. The older man usually hung out on the corner in front of the liquor store there. Weed-Eyes was always on the lookout for any kind of hustle, plus he owned a car. Don knew that for a small fee, it would be easy to convince him to chauffeur him around until he found something suitable to fill Monkeyhead's order.

The middle-aged crackhead was right where Don had guessed he would be—standing on the corner. Following his daily routine, Weed-Eyes was drinking wine, talking shit with his cronies, and keeping his green eyes peeled for his next opportunity to make a little dough.

Don hailed the tall, light-skinned hype. "Woody, what's up, my man? Check it out. Let me put this bug in your ear."

Pausing with the paper-bag-sheathed wine bottle halfway to his lips, Weed-Eyes considered Don's request. "Hold tight, little brother. Imma dig on what you got to say, but first let me knock the corners off this vino, you dig."

Not to be brushed off, Don said, "Man, fuck that vino. Nigga, I'm talkin 'bout lining yo pocket. I'll buy you a liter of Rosé, you just got to go in there and get it."

Weed-Eyes handed the bottle to one of the winos standing with him. He accepted the two dollars from Don and went in the store to buy the drink. He returned, drink in hand. He followed Don as they retreated to the middle of the block and took a seat on the abandoned carcass of a stripped car. Weed-Eyes broke the seal on the wine bottle and poured out a small amount. "For the cats that ain't here, you dig," he said, before taking a long swallow. He offered the bottle to Don, but he declined.

Don waited until Weed-Eyes got himself situated, then he started his pitch. "Imma get right down to business. I got pigeons lined up that want tires and sounds and shit like that, but they don't want to pay no store prices. I can get the merch. My only problem is that I don't got no kind of transportation. That's where you come in."

Weed-Eyes squinted at the sun. "So what you saying, little brother, is that you want ole Weed to fire up the heavy Chevy and take you out looking for a vic?"

"Yep, that's all there is to it," Don said. "I'll do the peeling, the stealing, and the wheeling."

Weed-Eyes asked, "So what the pay looking like?"

"Every night that we come up I'll hit you with a bill," Don answered.

Weed-Eyes choked on the wine he was swallowing when he heard Don's offer. "You got to be bullshitting. You mean to tell me that all I got to do is take you out, then make sure you get home alright, and I get a hundred bones for my troubles."

"Yep."

"That's righteous, little brother," Weed-Eyes commented. "When do we start?"

"Pick me up tonight at my crib at two in the morning."

In his room, Don gave Juanita instructions to wake him at two in the morning. Fully dressed he crawled into bed and went to sleep.

Promptly at two, Juanita shook him until he woke. Don cleared the cobwebs of sleep from his head with a hastily smoked rock. He grabbed his screwdriver and left the room. He sat on the front porch, smoking cigarettes and waiting for Weed-Eyes to arrive.

Fifteen minutes late, Weed-Eyes pulled to the curb in front of Don's house. The old, blue Chevy Citation was one headlight short, but other than that it seemed to be in good running condition. Don climbed into the passenger seat and

Weed-Eyes pulled off. The more distance they put between themselves and home, the better the neighborhoods looked.

They had been driving around in various neighborhoods for over forty-five minutes when Don put his hand on Weed-Eyes' arm. "Slow down," he ordered. Weed-Eyes complied. Excitement crept into Don's voice as he pointed. "Check that motherfucka out, right there! That cream-colored Bonneville right there! It's some fresh-looking thirties on that bitch, damn! Go 'round the block. Ain't even see no alarm light on it—just a fucking Club!"

Weed-Eyes circumnavigated the block. He slowed down to let Don out. Hands in his pocket, Don walked casually down the same side of the street as the Bonneville. He peered at the windows of the house that the car was parked in front of. He didn't detect any movement within, so he approached the car.

Using the flathead of the screwdriver, he popped the door lock out. With his finger he hit the mechanism to unlock the door. Again he used the screwdriver to break open the steering column on the left side. Next he tackled the Club. The owner had put it on upside down—a common mistake. He pulled and bent the steering wheel until he felt the Club give enough for him to wrench it off. He tossed the so-called theft deterrent on the passenger seat. He got a tight grip on the steering wheel and wrenched it back and forth until he felt it slacken up. He started the car by using his fingers to pull up the ignition lever until the car came to life. He slapped the Bonneville into gear and eased out of the parking space.

Running with the headlights out, he sped up the block. In the rearview mirror he could see Weed-Eyes bringing up the rear. Skillfully, Don handled the large car as he headed for the expressway. Don stopped for traffic lights only when it was absolutely necessary as he headed for home base. At every intersection his head swiveled back and forth looking for police. He didn't breathe a sigh of relief until they pulled into the vacant lot where they would strip the car of its rims and any other accessories he deemed valuable enough to take. The vacant lot was only a few blocks from Don's house, so if they had to make a quick getaway they only had to hop a few gates and they would be in Don's kitchen.

Weed-Eyes proved to be an asset as an accomplice. He handed Don a pair of work gloves, the one thing Don had forgotten, and they got down to business. The older crackhead worked alongside Don quickly and efficiently to help him remove the rims and tires. Don popped the trunk and they removed the amps and speakers. He couldn't find the snatch-out radio so he left the sleeve in the dashboard. Before getting out of the car, he took care to wipe the interior clean of any fingerprints. Leaving the stolen Bonneville sitting on milk crates and bricks, they headed for Don's house.

At Don's house, while Weed-Eyes waited on the porch, Don went inside to make the call. He dialed the number, and even though it was after four in the morning, Monkeyhead answered after four rings.

"Who this?" Monkeyhead asked.

"It's Don, nigga."

"Who?"

"Don-Don, man."

Recognition crept into Monkeyhead's voice. "Don, what the deal? What's up with you?"

"I got what we had talked about," Don said triumphantly. "Is you ready?"

Monkeyhead couldn't believe it. "Don, you bullshitting, nigga. What they look like?"

"These boys is clean as the board of health. Fat meat on the Vogues and the thirties is shining in the dark," Don said smugly. "What's up, you want to do this shit or not? 'Cause man, I can sell these motherfuckas anywhere."

"Don't do no shit like that, Don," Monkeyhead said, a note of anxiety creeping into his voice. "Come over to Harper Court. I got the scratch. Bring the rims. Is that cool?"

Don paused a moment before answering. He had Monkeyhead right where he wanted him. It was time to discuss price. "Monkey, these motherfuckas is clean, with brand-new tires. Imma need at least a gee for these boys."

"Don, I ain't tripping on the price, I just want to see the merch. Man, bring the shit through Harper. I'm out here."

Don ran upstairs, grabbed his pistol, and they left.

At Harper Court, even though it was four in the morning, it was business as usual. The only difference was at night the dealers openly displayed their weaponry. Monkeyhead was right where he said he would be. He walked up to Weed-Eyes' car with a Tech-9 slung on his shoulder.

Warily, Weed-Eyes unlocked the trunk of his car while keeping his eyes on the fierce-looking youth. Monkeyhead noticed the way Weed-Eyes was staring at the semiautomatic firearm.

"Don't trip 'bout the heat," Monkeyhead told them. "Late nights you got to have you some protection, you know."

Monkeyhead's explanation seemed to allay some of Weed-Eyes' uneasiness, but not by much. Stepping out of the way, Weed-Eyes let Monkeyhead inspect the merchandise in his trunk.

Monkeyhead's face broke into a wide grin at the sight of the rims. The elated dealer dug into his pocket and pulled out a rubber-band–wrapped knot. "Damn, Don! These motherfuckas right here gone have my shit looking cold! Hell yeah!" He handed the money to Don and called for a few of his fellow workers to help him get the rims out of the trunk.

Don stood back smiling, but all the while watching every movement Monkeyhead made.

"I don't need to count this, do I?" Don asked as he climbed back into the passenger seat. He handed Monkeyhead three hundred dollars. "Have one of yo guys bring me a quarter onion and a ball."

Monkeyhead slammed the trunk when the last rim was removed, then he walked to the passenger door. "Nigga, you better count it," he said jokingly.

Don laughed as he took the rubber band off the money

and began to count it. "Before I forget, you don't need no music, do you? I got some amps and speakers and shit."

"I don't need shit," Monkeyhead said, leaning on the car door. "But hold off on selling that shit if you can. My nigga Sajak was just talking 'bout getting some music and shit for his ride. I forgot that nigga new cell number, but the minute I see that stud I'll let him know that you got some merch."

One of the dealers walked to the car, leaned down into the passenger window, and dropped a quarter-ounce and eightball of crack into Don's lap. Don gave Weed-Eyes the signal to start the car.

"Get my number off yo phone if you need to hit me," Don said, leaning out the window as Weed-Eyes pulled off. "If anybody else need some rims for they car let me know. I'm like Pizza Hut, I deliver."

Monkeyhead stood watching them drive away with a smile on his face.

In the car, Don dropped five twenty-dollar bills on the seat beside Weed-Eyes. He broke open the eightball of crack and pinched Weed-Eyes off a nice piece.

"I know I only told you I was gone give you a bill," Don explained, "but shit, you held me down. So, I'm gone hold you down."

Weed-Eyes smiled. "Thanks, little brother, you dig. You got my help anytime."

"We gone hit them again, real soon. Take me to the crib, the motherfucking sun is 'bout to come up."

"Hey, baby, how did things go?" she asked anxiously.

"It was cool," Don said as he waved the six hundred dollars and tossed the quarter-ounce of crack on the bed.

Juanita scooped it up like a Cubs shortstop. "I love you, Don. You always manage to get yo hands on that butter. When you came in I was just thinking."

Don had pulled off his shirt and was sitting on the edge of the bed preparing to take a hit of crack. "What was you thinking?"

Juanita came around to Don's side of the bed. She kneeled on the floor in front of him and took the torch from his hand. She lit it and held it to the bowl of the hooter for him. Don laid back on the bed and blew crack smoke toward the ceiling.

Juanita took the pipe from his hand. "Baby, I was thinking that it got kind of boring with just the two of us sitting here smoking all day. I think we need some company."

"What is you talking 'bout, girl?"

"I'm just saying that we got a nice little piece of crack and we can afford to kick it."

"Kick it with who?"

"With my friend."

"Who is yo friend?"

"Her name is Wanda. She live over there on Cottage Grove in the walk-ups."

"How you know her?"

"She my brother's baby's mama. She real cool. That's my girl and I miss kicking it with her. If you don't want her to come over here, then you can give me a little piece and I can go over there for a few."

Don thought about it. He really didn't want to let her out of his sight and he had to admit that it was growing a bit boring just sitting there looking at each other while they smoked. "I don't give a fuck. She can come through."

"She probably have her man with her," she hedged out. "He ain't no problem, though. If she don't bring him, then she probably can't come. He be on some bullshit. He ain't like you; he all jealous and shit."

"Whatever, they just better act like they got some sense while they up in my crib."

Juanita made a brief telephone call and fifteen minutes later there was a female voice calling her name in the backyard. She went downstairs and escorted the couple upstairs to Don's attic bedroom.

Juanita gave a brief introduction. "Don, this is my girl, Wanda. She my motherfucking girl," Juanita said happily as she slapped hands with Wanda. Her voice was dry as she said, "And this is her man, Raoul."

Raoul stuck out his hand. For a moment it seemed that Don wouldn't show him any love, but finally he shook the older man's hand. As they took a seat Don surveyed the pair with disdain. Wanda was about average height with ninety-degree-angle hips and shriveled breasts that were all too visible in a halter top several times her size. Raoul was a beanpole of a man. Something about his ferretlike countenance made Don distrust him right away. The way Raoul's eyes scanned the room made Don feel like Raoul was doing a mental inventory of things to steal. When he was sure that they weren't paying attention, Don slid over to his dresser and stuffed his pistol in his waistband.

The more he thought about it, the more he didn't want the two hypes in his bedroom. Calmly but firmly he insisted that they move the festivities to the garage.

In the garage, Juanita and Wanda chitchatted while Don cleaned off an old card table to put the pipe and mirror on.

When he dumped some crack on a mirror from the quarter ounce, all conversation stopped. Wanda and Raoul had hoped to smoke only a dime bag or two, but the amount of crack on the mirror challenged their crack-hungering minds. As if by magic, Wanda's pipe appeared in her hand, but Don ignored her.

They all watched Don take a long, leisurely hit, then pass the pipe to Juanita. Don took a razor blade and slid about a twenty-dollar-bag worth from the big pile for Wanda and Raoul.

"Y'all two gone get down with that there," Don told them.

For a few seconds it appeared as if the couple would come to blows over which one of them would get the first hit when Wanda sat forward and put a few chips of crack in her pipe.

Raoul said, "Damn, why you always get to take the first bust?"

"Fuck you, Raoul," Wanda hissed. "Don't be starting up in here. Shit, we got a motherfucking dub of yay right here and you crying about who get the first bump. That's some petty shit if I ever heard it."

Don watched both of them with an amused look on his face.

Raoul was doing his best to control his temper. "I know the fuck you ain't trying to front me off in front of this nigga in his motherfucking garage. I ain't petty. I'm just saying is all. This here is sposed to be a party that we was both invited to. Being that we was both invited, I want to know why the fuck you gots to be the one that get the first hit?"

Before Wanda put the pipe to her lips, she said, "See, now you always got to show people just how stupid you is. Since you is not getting the shit, I'm gone break it down for you like you two years old: Because it's my gotdamn pipe. Not ours, or yours. Mine. Then the second reason is that Juanita invited us over here and she is my friend, not yours. So now that I done had to explain some shit to you that you shoulda knew, can I take my hit now?"

Wanda didn't wait for Raoul's answer. She put the pipe to her lips and flicked a torch. The good crack made her swoon a little bit. On purpose she took her time before handing the pipe to Raoul.

Don made a mental promise that he and Juanita would never turn out to be like the couple sitting across from them.

Wanda and Raoul smoked the piece Don had given them in about ten minutes. While Juanita and Don continued to smoke, Raoul and Wanda pretended to clean their pipe, but spent more time watching the younger couple than anything.

"Don," Wanda said.

He looked up, blowing crack smoke toward the ceiling. "What's up?"

Raoul pushed her shoulder. "Gone head and ask him, girl."

Wanda turned on Raoul. "Why don't you shut the fuck up!" she told Raoul.

"Bitch, just gone head and ask, shit," Raoul grumbled.

Wanda turned back to Don with a phony smile on her face. "Sorry 'bout that, Don. I just wanted to ask, you know, if we could get a little more."

"No," Don said casually. "I done already gave you motherfuckas a twinkie. Y'all didn't even say thank you for that shit. Matter of fact, why don't y'all get the fuck out of my house."

Raoul jumped to his feet. "Nigga, you ain't got to talk to my woman like that! Who the fuck you think you is, you young-ass punk!"

Nonchalantly, Don raised his T-shirt to show the butt of his pistol. "Man, you better calm yo thin ass down in my motherfucking house, dude. Now like I was saying before, get the fuck out of my damn house before I have yo skinny ass wearing a shit bag. Juanita, show them out."

Wanda and Raoul grumbled all the while as they followed Juanita out of the garage door and out into the alley.

"I'll call you, girl," Juanita whispered to Wanda as she closed the back gate behind the vexed couple. She had heard Don leaving the garage.

"You ain't have to put them out like that," she said when they were face-to-face.

"Girl, fuck them!" Don said. "Them motherfuckas just want to sit up and smoke up a nigga yams. They got to be crazy thinking Imma set out all my yay. Shit, when we struggling them motherfuckas ain't gone call us and have a smoke-out. Now bring yo ass on. I want some head."

"Un-uh, nigga. It's yo turn to lick my pussy while I take me a bump."

"I just might do that, shorty."

Don took her hand and led her upstairs to his bedroom.

DON DECIDED TO TAKE JUANITA SHOPPING—SOMETHING
he hadn't considered doing in a long time. He could use
some new shoes and Juanita was long overdue for some new
clothes. He took care to put on some clean socks before they
left, something his father had taught him he was always supposed to do if he was going to buy some new shoes. It was
funny how something his father had taught him so long ago
remained with him.

They found Weed-Eyes on his favorite corner.

"Weedy, what's happening with you, dog?" Don said by
way of greeting.

"Nothing much, youngblood. Just trying to put a couple
of dollars in the same pocket as always."

"Problem solved," Don announced as he started heading

toward Weed-Eyes' car. "We need a ride out to Evergreen Plaza so we can grab some stomps and a few outfits and shit. If you ain't too busy I'll give you some gas money and put a couple in yo pocket for a ride."

"Let's ride," Weed-Eyes said.

At the Plaza, Don and Juanita looked like a normal couple as they shopped. Weed-Eyes chose to remain in his car, reading his newspaper and drinking his wine. Two hours passed and the teenagers returned to the car, carrying a gang of bags and smiling.

Starting up the car, Weed-Eyes asked, "Where to, young-blood?"

Don had eaten a steak sandwich in the mall's food court and was feeling full and tired. "Run us by the crib. I got to get me a few hours, of sleep 'cause I want to go out tonight and take care of business. You gone be ready for tonight?"

"If I ain't then my eyes ain't green."

Weed-Eyes dropped them off at the house. Don hit him twenty-five dollars and they went inside as he pulled off.

Don stripped down to his boxer shorts and was almost asleep when the doorbell rang. He tried to ignore it, but whoever it was insisted that someone answer the door.

Don pulled on a T-shirt and a pair of shorts. Downstairs he looked out the window to see who was on the porch. Monkeyhead was pressing the doorbell again. Alongside him stood a boy Don recognized as Sajak.

Don unlocked the door and held open the screen door.

"Monkeyhead, Sajak. I was just about to knock some zs. What's up?"

Monkeyhead said, "Don, my fault, bruh. I told this nigga Sajak about that shit you got and he wanted me to bring him through yo crib."

"Alright, give me a minute to get the shit."

Don let the screen door slam and bounded up the stairs to his room. He stacked the stereo components on top of the kicker box. Before leaving his room, he grabbed his pistol and stuck it in his pocket. Better to be safe than sorry.

On the porch he let Sajak inspect the equipment. Almost immediately Sajak offered him four hundred dollars for the sounds. Not one to haggle over price, Don accepted the money.

Speaking in a voice cracking under the strain of puberty, Sajak said, "Monkeyhead showed me them thirties you got him. I got a Regal, a clean one. I want some racing rims for it. Some Billets or something. My shit in the pipe shop right now. When I get it out, I want to take it to the sound shop to put this shit in there. Now all I got to buy is a CD player. Man, do you think you could get them rims for me?"

Don chuckled self-confidently. "Nigga, if you wanted wagon wheels I could get them. You just make sure that you have that scratch ready 'cause I'll be to see you. And don't worry about no CD player neither. I'll track one down for you."

"I ain't tripping on the money. I don't give a fuck long as the rims is clean. And please make sure that they got some nice meat on the tires. Oh yeah, and if you can try to make sure that you get all the rim caps."

Don yawned and stretched his tired limbs. "Alright, shorty, I got it. Thanks for shopping at Don-Don's discount auto parts, but like I said before, I was about to knock some zs."

———

That night Don hit the streets with Weed-Eyes in search of some racing rims for Sajak. In the middle of the block on 78th and Hermitage, Weed-Eyes spotted a navy-blue Cutlass sitting on Billets.

"Little brother," Weed-Eyes said, "check out that Cutlass right there."

Don agreed he had found what they needed. After cruising the block twice to make sure that everything was quiet, Weed-Eyes dropped Don on the corner.

When Don got close to the car he saw the red warning light mounted above the dashboard that meant the car had an alarm. That didn't deter him—it was a simple matter to bypass them. Using his screwdriver, Don broke the driver's side taillight. He stuck the rubber-handled tool into the remainder of the broken bulb in the socket to complete the circuit and make the alarm short itself out. The alarm system gave two halfhearted chirps and the dashboard warning light indicator faded. He popped the door lock out and had the car started in under two minutes. Following the same routine as the night before, Don was nosing the steamer in the vacant lot twenty minutes later. He parked it alongside the Bonneville that had donated Monkeyhead's rims. With Weed-Eyes' help the four rims were off the Cutlass twenty minutes later. The custom steering wheel had the same design as the rims, so Don stole that too. While Weed-Eyes was arranging the rims in his trunk, Don popped the trunk of the steamer.

Inside was a huge kickerbox with two twelve-inch sub-woofers, four six-by-nines, two amplifiers, and a crossover. Don speedily severed the wires of the components and snatched them out. Inside the car he found the snatch-out radio under the driver's seat and an equalizer mounted under the dashboard.

Don was so frantic with their haul that he didn't go home to call Monkeyhead. They headed straight for Harper Court. It was an easy task to find Sajak. The boy was waiting, hoping that Don was coming that night. He was overjoyed with the rims, matching steering wheel, and CD player.

Sajak paid him for the rims and Don had Weed-Eyes drop him off at home.

At home, after taking a generous hit of crack, Don relaxed while Juanita tinkered with the car stereo components he had brought home. She was examining the speakers when she discovered something.

"Don, baby, come look at this. There's something in there."

Cut into the side of the kickerbox were holes that let the speakers "breathe." Don put his eye to the hole and could just make out some type of package.

"Damn, girl, you ain't lying. There is something in this motherfucka. Reach in that drawer and hand me that Phillips screwdriver."

Don unscrewed and removed the speaker cover and the woofer. He reached into the box and pulled out the package. It was wrapped in brown paper and secured with masking tape. As if it were a Christmas present he tore the wrapper open. The next layer was a balloonlike substance. He ripped a hole in it. Another layer of thick packaging was underneath the rubber. He ripped through the plastic using the screwdriver's tip.

Juanita had taken a seat on the bed and was hitting the pipe.

"Juanita, come here," Don whispered in awe.

With the pipe still in her hand, Juanita crossed the room and stood by Don's shoulder. Curiously she looked at him as he looked at the package.

"Baby," he said, his voice still barely above a whisper. "This is a motherfucking kilo of cocaine."

Using the fingernail of his baby finger Don scraped some powder off the brick and tasted it.

"Baby, this is cocaine. Taste this shit."

She obeyed and came to the same conclusion—cocaine.

On instinct Don stuck his hand back inside the yawning hole in the speaker box and felt around. His hand rubbed against another package and he pulled it out. It was another package wrapped exactly the same as the first.

Don took a seat on the floor beside the kickerbox. He had to think. This was too good to be true. He knew that there was a drug dealer somewhere kicking himself in the ass for hiding two kilos in his car. *Fuck you very much for the two keys,* he said to himself.

To Juanita's astonishment, Don broke out into wild laughter and continued laughing until tears were rolling down his cheeks.

TEMPTATION TO TRY AND SMOKE THE BETTER PORTION OF the kilos was great, but Don resisted the urge; fear of a massive coronary prevented him from indulging too heavily. The cocaine was the best he had consumed in his short career as a clucker. It gave him the feeling of being superhuman—smarter, stronger, and cooler than everyone else.

Still, he had problems.

Not the ordinary problems that most crackheads are faced with, like the lack of money or crack. Don's problems stemmed from having too much cocaine. Never in his young life did he realize just how much cocaine a kilo actually was. It was way too much cocaine for personal use. The only logical thing to do was sell it. That led to another problem. Don didn't have the clientele to try and sell weight, plus he knew from experience that he didn't have the patience it took to build a clientele list.

The more he thought about it, he concluded that his only option was to try and unload one or both of the kilos. The only person he knew he could try and sell a kilo to was Diego. He seriously doubted the half-breed had the currency to purchase both of them.

He glanced over at Juanita. She was sprawled across the bed, finally passed out after a night of smoking crack. The soles of her small feet were filthy from walking around barefoot. He couldn't recall her getting in the tub or shower in the last forty-eight hours. *Damn, she looking whupped,* he thought, *Imma have to hurry up and get this shit away from her before she OD in this motherfucka.* Her once-luscious figure was quickly going out the window. She had become a total slob—never wanting to cook or clean the room. Lately it seemed the only thing that got her out of bed was crack. Ever since the night she discovered the kilos in the speaker box, she had been smoking like a broken stove. When he tried to slow her down she would pout for awhile or suck his dick until he conceded. To him it seemed that if she didn't have the glass dick in her mouth, it was his dick. Old-fashioned sex had almost became non-existent, only oral sex to get her way.

At first his mother had protested about her staying there, but since she seemed to keep him in the house, she didn't put up too much of a fuss. His mother acted like she almost liked Juanita.

Don was starting to look at Juanita in a different light and it wasn't a good one. He said to himself, *when I get rid of this shit, I'm gone have to get rid of this bitch. With all the paper I'm gone have, I can find me a new bitch. One that don't fuck around with this crack shit.*

That was a matter for another day—one day soon, though. Right now, he needed to make an important telephone call. Downstairs in the living room he found the telephone and picked it up. He dialed the number from his head, but when he held it to his ear he could hear his sister.

"I'm on the damn phone!" Rhonda yelled into the receiver.

"Well get the fuck off!" he said harshly.

"I ain't getting off nothing! This ain't yo phone, boy!"

He calmed down. "Girl, yo always on the damn phone, shit. I just want to make a quick call, then you can get right back on the motherfucka."

"Girl, I'll call you back in a minute," his sister said to her friend and hung up.

Don dialed the number again. "Diego, my man, what's up?"

"Who this?" Diego asked warily.

"Don-Don, nigga."

"What's up Don. We working. Come through the Court."

"I ain't on that shit, Diego. I need you to come through my crib real quick, so we can talk business."

"What's up?" Diego asked suspiciously.

"Nigga, it's all good. Come through my tip. Believe me, you don't want to miss out on this one."

"Alright, I'll be there in about twenty minutes."

"Make it ten."

"Cool."

To prepare himself for the meeting with Diego, Don smoked a healthy rock in his bedroom.

The sound of the crack sizzling in the pipe woke Juanita. She sat up like a zombie and tried to snatch the pipe from his hand. They scuffled, resulting in Don's favorite pipe sailing across the room and shattering against the wall. A glass shard rebounded and embedded in Don's forearm. With a howl of pain he snatched the glass from his arm. A rivulet of blood ran down his arm and dripped onto the carpet.

Totally pissed off, Don rained blows on Juanita's head and shoulders. She tried to grab his flailing arms and they both fell off the bed. Don scrambled to his feet and stomped her head into the carpet until she stopped moving.

He went to the bathroom to clean his wound cursing all the while. He went back to his bedroom with a towel wrapped around the deep puncture in his forearm. In his room he retrieved his cigarette and a sample bag of cocaine. He ignored Juanita's crumpled form as he stepped over her and made his way downstairs to wait on the porch for Diego.

Twenty minutes later, Diego's Chevy Blazer pulled up to the curb in front of Don's house. Along with Diego, Sajak and Lonnie disembarked from the sport utility vehicle. They stepped up onto the porch and exchanged greetings with Don.

Diego took a seat on the porch banister. "Don, baby boy. What's so important that you needed me to come over here? It better be good 'cause you taking me away from my hustle."

"Diego, this is Don-Don you talking to. Shit, nigga, I'm a hustler too, so you know that this shit got to be 'bout some cash. I wanted to holla at you 'cause you the moneyman around this motherfucka. I got a sweet deal for you. Is you interested?"

"I wouldn'ta came over here if I wasn't interested, nigga. Spit it out."

Taking his time, Don blew cigarette smoke into the gentle breeze. "What if I told you that I got my hands on a cake of the best yayo this side of Colombia."

"Bullshit," Lonnie said.

Don looked at him like he was a child that had spoken out of turn; he had never liked Lonnie much. "I'm talking to the boss," he said. "You just the hired help so when I'm talking to the boss, please don't interrupt." He turned back to Diego. "The shit is soft, untouched. It's so good that a chef could bounce this shit back to at least a cake and a half. The shit is ready to be delivered. All you got to do is say the motherfucking word."

"Hold on, Don. If ole Diego don't know shit else, he know that if something sound too good to be true, then it usually is. That's just the nature of the game. Answer three questions, then I'll know that yo fo' real."

"Shoot," Don said confidently.

"How do I know that the coke is really that good? If it is, when can we see the whole slab? And last, but certainly not least, how much is you talking for the whole book?"

Undaunted, Don pulled the sample bag from his pocket. "You know this game is cold but it's fair, Diego, but since you niggas is alright with me, I'm gone give y'all a sweet deal. See, you held me down when I was in a tight spot a couple of times and I ain't gone forget that shit. For twenty gees the key is yours. Here's a sample of it." He tossed the Baggie to Diego. "Take you a bump to see what's to it. I'm telling you that the shit I got in my hands is good to go. There's a piece of crack I cooked up from the shit in there too, so you can have one of the geekers take a hit."

Don watched Diego take a snort from the bag and then hand it to Lonnie, who took a snort also. Sajak declined.

Diego was the first to speak. His voice was gravelly from the raw cocaine in his throat. "Damn, Don. That shit taste like butter. If you got a key of that shit there, it's all good. Why don't you give us a minute to crunch the numbers."

"Ain't no thang. I'll be in the crib. Just ring the bell when you niggas is ready to talk business."

Don left the porch while the three dealers held a conference.

Diego's face was frozen. He took another snort from the

Baggie. "Man, this is better shit than we copped the last three times we went to the store. If this nigga got a cake of this shit, we could drop a half a kilo of B-12 on this shit and it would still be better than the shit we got."

Lonnie agreed. "You ain't lying, man. That shit would pump the set straight up. Cluckers would be coming from everywhere like when we had that shit from Kody and them before the feds got they ass."

Diego said, "You ain't never lied. But I ain't about to give no hype twenty gees of my scratch." He motioned for Lonnie and Sajak to come closer. "Man, we could take this nigga's shit," he whispered, his voice still raspy from the raw cocaine. "Don don't be with Big Man and them no more, so he ain't got nobody to ride for him. Why the fuck should we scrape up twenty gees when we can just make this nigga cough this shit up? That is if the nigga really got a whole key."

Lonnie was charged—as much by the cocaine as the thought of conspiracy. "Hell, yeah! Fuck this stud. I hate this nigga anyway. Shit, I'm with this shit. I'd pop the dog shit out of my auntie for a kilo of this coke!"

Both Diego and Lonnie looked at Sajak. He was the youngest and most inexperienced among them. The youngster sorely wanted to live up to the thug image.

"What you say, Sajak?" Diego asked.

Sajak patted his short afro. "Whatever, yo. I don't give a fuck. I mean if this nigga do got a whole key of cola and it's as good as y'all say it is then we needs that."

Diego walked over and rang the doorbell. "Bet, we gone take this nigga shit. When this nigga come back out just follow my lead. Act like everything is all good."

When Diego rang the doorbell, Don was upstairs smoking a rock on a pipe considerably less elaborate than the work of art Juanita had broken. Exhaling the white-hot smoke from his lungs, Don went downstairs. Before he opened the door and stepped on the porch he tried to compose himself.

His efforts were to no avail.

The three drug dealers knew from the sweaty, geeked look on his face that he had just smoked some crack. Mentally, Diego chalked themselves a point.

Diego said, "We discussed it and it sounds like you got yo'self a deal. We'll buy it from you tonight. All we need is a meeting place where we all will feel comfortable. You can pick the spot, Don."

Don mopped the beaded sweat on his forehead. "Down on St. Lawrence. You know that big abandoned building in the middle of the block? Be in the back of that motherfucka at twelve tonight. If y'all not there by one minute after twelve then I'm gone."

Lonnie was so happy that the unsuspecting Don walked into their trap he almost laughed, but a chilling glance from Diego made him straighten up. Still, he couldn't resist making a small threat. "Don, I hope yo ass ain't playing no games 'cause it'll get real ugly. If shit be looking shady I ain't gone hesitate to melt a motherfucka!"

Don laughed at Lonnie's threat. "Don't even trip, nigga. I ain't finta play with no nigga either. Especially when it come down to a whole kilo. So I advise you niggas not to be acting shady. Just be the fuck on time or like I said I'm gone thin out."

Don shook hands with the three dealers signaling that the meeting had came to a satisfactory end. He stood on the porch and watched them climb into the Blazer and roar away.

They got to be on some new shit that I ain't even tried yet if they think that I would trust them with a slab, he thought. They didn't know it yet, but he had the whole thing mapped out. He wasn't insane enough to try and control a transaction of this magnitude by himself. He needed a mule. And the only person he could halfway trust was Weed-Eyes.

He took one more look up and down the block before he went inside the house, letting the screen door slam.

JUANITA SHOOK DON TO AWAKEN HIM. HE COULD TELL from the wide-eyed look on her face she had been smoking crack since he went to sleep hours ago. He started to whup her ass again, but he was already a little behind schedule, so he postponed it.

He dressed rapidly and took himself a quick hit. His new pipe was still warm to the touch from Juanita's use. Grabbing the bag with the kilo in it, his pistol, and a few extra rounds, Don left the house. At a dead sprint he headed for the abandoned building on St. Lawrence.

Don was in a good mood. He was slightly apprehensive about making such a large transaction, but the thought of acquiring $20,000 eased the tension. As he ran, his thoughts touched on the fact that he was broke—begging for credit a few weeks ago, but now he was about to come up. When he saw Weed-Eyes sitting in his car a block from the meeting place he slowed down to a walk. He walked over to the car and got in.

Weed-Eyes looked over at Don. He noticed Don's bucked eyes and smelled the burned crack in Don's clothes. "What's up, little brother. You a little early. Man, I hope you brought some of that good shit you been smoking with you."

Don smiled and sat the kilo on the car seat between them. "As a matter of fact I did, Weedy."

Don pulled a plastic bag out of his pocket with a little over two-and-a-half ounces of cooked cocaine in it. The only reason he was carrying such a large piece was because he had been afraid to leave it around Juanita. The way she smoked, leaving that much crack around her was almost assuredly a death sentence. Don dug into his pocket and pulled out a six-inch length of antenna he had broken off the television in his mother's room. He pinched a small piece of crack from the bag and placed it on the steel wool shoved into the largest end of the antenna. With his lighter he melted the rock to hold it in place. He placed the end of the antenna wrapped with masking tape to his lips. He held the lighter to it and inhaled. Satisfied with his hit, he handed the straight-shooter to Weed-Eyes and gave him a crack rock.

Weed-Eyes skillfully followed the same procedure.

"Damn, little brother," he exclaimed, as he blew the

crack smoke out of his nostrils. "That's some good smoke. Definitely that butter. That's better than the shit they be having over there on Harper. When this deal is over, I'm gone cop me a ball of that shit and take it out west to this bitch name Rachel crib. This little freak bitch will suck the sleeve off a nigga swipe for a hit of this good cola. Probably rent me a room for about a week and keep my swilla down the bitch throat."

Don laughed, then turned serious. "Yeah, that shit sound like a plan, but you got to put that shit out yo mind right now. Think about the shit that's about to go down. I picked this building 'cause me and my homies used to haunt this motherfucka. I know it inside and out. The shit is gone go down in the back. Right in the middle of the backyard is a Dumpster. It's still there—I checked. Keep the Dumpster between you and them studs."

Weed-Eyes interrupted. "Little brother, you don't think them cats is gone try to rip us off, do you?"

"I don't know," Don replied. "But if they do, I'll be ready for the shit, so don't trip. Just do like I say and keep the Dumpster between y'all. You won't see me, but I'll be there. Let them studs know right off the top ain't nothing moving until you see the money. If shit look like it finta get shady, I would advise you to duck." To emphasize his words Don pulled his .357 from his waistband.

Weed-Eyes got out of the car and headed for the abandoned building. Don gave him a head start, then got out too.

He walked over a block, cut through a gangway, and stealthily ducked into the garage behind the abandoned building. On tiptoe he picked his way through the rubble of a partially caved-in roof. He peered through a hole in the wall that once had a window. From his vantage point he could see Weed-Eyes sitting on the overturned Dumpster. He watched his mule pull a wine bottle shrouded with a paper bag from his back pocket and take a swig.

Don stepped back into the shadows. He wanted a cigarette, but he knew the brief minute it would take to light one could give away his position if someone was watching. He knew that it was almost twelve and Diego would be showing in a moment. When he leaned against the garage wall to resign himself to waiting he heard a sound. It sounded like someone kicking glass.

Don quieted his breathing and cocked his ears in the wind like a dog. He heard it again—he was right, those were footsteps. Someone was trying to be quiet, but failing miserably.

For a brief moment a figure stood in the garage's mouth, then slipped into the interior shadows. The figure moved fast, but not before Don identified the silhouette as Sajak. The young boy was carrying what Don guessed was a shotgun.

Don knew that although Sajak was carrying a shotty it didn't have to mean it was a setup. He might just be there to have Diego's back. Don watched Sajak walk over to the hole in the wall. Sajak took position there.

Whatever the case, Don knew from his position he could easily overcome Sajak. For now he would just wait and see how the deal went down.

Not twelve feet from where Sajak was standing, Don watched Diego and Lonnie saunter into the yard.

Diego walked up to Weed-Eyes with a smile on his face before he realized in the dim light it wasn't Don. The smile dropped off his lips and he scanned the yard suspiciously. He swung his gaze back to rest on Weed-Eyes. "Nigga, clear out of here. I got business to tend to. You gots to find somewhere else to get cracked up, bruh."

"You Diego, ain't you?" Weed-Eyes asked timidly.

"Why?"

"Because I'm supposed to wait here for you. Don said that you would be here at twelve."

Diego wasn't satisfied with Weed-Eyes' answer. "Nigga, I ain't got no time to be fucking around with no motherfucking messenger boy! Where the fuck is Don at?"

Weed-Eyes tried to lighten the situation. "Behind that preposition."

"Man, what the fuck is you bumping about, dude?"

"Nothing, nothing," Weed-Eyes said. "Little brother, ain't no reason for you to get all stressed out, you dig. Don had another customer to meet so he told me to meet you here. You got the scratch?"

Diego thought for a moment he had been outwitted by Don, but it dawned on him that the man before him had to have the kilo. Now he just had to get his hands on it.

Much calmer, Diego said, "Yeah, I got the cash. Do you got the key?"

"I got the cola right here, but I can't give it to you until I check out the paper, little brother."

Diego looked around. *This is too sweet,* he thought.

"Lonnie, give this stud the shoe box," Diego ordered.

With a wicked grin on his face, Lonnie walked over to the Dumpster and placed a Timberland shoe box on it. He flipped the lid open. Neatly arranged in the box were rubber-band-wrapped bundles of money. There was a hundred-dollar bill on top of each one.

"Each one of them stacks is five gees," Diego said, while Lonnie leered in Weed-Eyes' face.

Watching Lonnie with one eye, Weed-Eyes checked through the bundles to make sure none of the stacks were funny. Everything looked legit, so Weed-Eyes removed the kilo from the front of his pants and slid it across the Dumpster to Lonnie.

Using the edge of a straight razor, Lonnie cut a corner of the plastic wrapping of the kilo and scraped a bit off. He snorted it heartily. He turned to his boss. "Yeah, baby. This is the same shit. Uhh, it's good. If we really had to spend that twenty on this shit, I wouldn't mind too much." Lonnie snorted and spit. "Nall, I'm lying."

Bewildered at Lonnie's comment, Weed-Eyes asked, "What you mean *if,* little brother? You done already paid for the cola, you dig."

The two laughed as if Weed-Eyes had told a side-clutching

joke. When they finally stopped laughing both of them pulled out pistols.

It happened so fast that Weed-Eyes didn't realize the deal had gone south until he was looking into the business end of Lonnie's 9-millimeter. Hoping Don was watching as he had promised, Weed-Eyes tried to speak, but he was so afraid his throat locked up on him. To try and calm himself, Weed-Eyes picked up his wine bottle off the Dumpster and took a sip.

"Slow down, little brothers," Weed-Eyes said, once he was able to control his voice again. "What's up with the pistol play?"

Diego sneered, "You know what this is, hype. We should take yo life, but we only gone take the coke."

In the garage, Don was silently making his move on Sajak. With the fluidity of a boa constrictor Don stole up behind the wannabe thug and slipped his arm around Sajak's neck. After trapping his throat in wiry biceps Don tapped his temple with the .357.

"Nigga, if you fart loud Imma knock yo shit out yo head," Don hissed in Sajak's ear, keeping one eye on the proceedings in the yard. "Lose that shotgun and do it quietly, bitch. If I hear a clatter, yo brains gone scatter."

Sajak carefully laid the shotgun down.

"Now walk, bitch. And take it slow before I air condition yo motherfucking head."

Don's arm was still around Sajak's neck as he maneuvered him into the yard. Diego's boasting subsided as his mouth fell open at Don's sudden appearance. The look of fear etched on Lonnie's face was unmistakable. The cocky drug dealer's hand shook as he pointed his pistol at Don.

Don was pissed off. "So you niggas think y'all slick! Ain't this a bitch! Y'all already got money and trying to stick a motherfucka up! Weedy, grab that shoe box and the yay and go get in the car. You niggas back the fuck up or I'll blow this nigga shit loose!"

Don didn't have to tell them twice; four pairs of eyes watched Weed-Eyes collect the shoe box and the kilo. Moving like a scalded dog, Weed-Eyes left the yard and headed for his car.

Once he was safely behind the wheel of his vehicle, Weed-Eyes analyzed the situation. In his lap was the cocaine and the twenty thousand dollars, Don was still in the backyard—alone, outmanned, and outgunned. There was no way of predicting the outcome of this one. With that in mind, Weed-Eyes did the logical thing: He started his car, put it in drive, and headed for the West Side.

Unaware of his companion's treachery, Don was negotiating for Sajak's life.

"Spic-ass nigga, you think this a joke, don't you? Back the fuck up!" Don snarled through clenched teeth.

Smiling, Diego tried to throw Don off the scent. "Don, my man. Slow the gorilla role, baby boy. We was just fucking around with yo man. We wadn't gone really rob the old dude. It was just a joke, you know what I mean. Don't even trip—we can all walk out of here. Just drop our package off at Harper Court and there's no hard feelings."

"Nigga, who the fuck do you think I am?" Don sneered. "You bitches . . ."

Don never got a chance to finish his sentence as Lonnie fired his pistol at Don's head. Lonnie thought he was a marksman, but the closest the shot came to Don was going through Sajak's temple. Brain matter, blood, and skull fragments showered Don.

Still using Sajak's lifeless body for a shield, Don, his face a mask of determination, swung his gun in Lonnie's and Diego's direction. Diego's pistol spit several rounds. Two of them hit Sajak's body, making Don take a few steps back to lessen the impact of the slugs thudding home into his makeshift shield. In response to Diego, Don let off the six shots in his pistol at both men. He dropped Sajak's body and dove into the garage to reload his pistol.

One of Don's slugs tore through Lonnie's stomach. Clutching his belly, Lonnie sprinted from the backyard, through the gangway, and out to the street. Once he gained St. Lawrence, he kept running as blood flowed over his fingertips. He tossed his pistol into some weeds and kept going.

Diego shot the remaining rounds of his clip into the garage hoping to hit Don with a lucky shot. The only problem was Don wasn't in the garage. He had knelt and filled his pistol with fresh ammo and ducked out of the garage. Quickly and quietly he made his way past the garage to the small corridor that ran between that one and another abandoned garage. Cutting through the gangway brought him back into the yard, behind Diego, who was ducked down behind the Dumpster inserting a fresh clip in his pistol.

"Diego, drop that pistol, bitch!" Don commanded from behind him.

Diego started to turn to fire, but Don sensed his movement before he could make it and shot him in the right arm. Diego's pistol clattered to the concrete.

The pain from the half-inch hole in his arm was excruciating. Don kicked Diego's pistol away from him. It slid along the concrete and came to a halt about ten feet away. Don already knew what he had to do. He firmly planted his feet in front of Diego. He put his hand to his eyes to shield them from the inevitable blood spray and put his pistol to Diego's head.

Diego looked up at Don. All the contempt was erased from his countenance; only the pitiful face of a scared boy remained.

"Don, hold up," Diego whimpered. "Please don't kill me. I'll give you anything you want. My truck, money, my crib, whatever. Please don't kill me. If you let me live, I'll walk out of here and you'll never see me again, I swear."

Don lowered his arm and considered Diego's pleas. He had to admit the boy sounded sincere, but Don knew it wasn't in his best interest to leave him alive. It was an unwritten, ageless rule of the streets: Don't leave your enemies alive if you want to live longer than they do.

"Ain't no reason to beg, nigga. You said it yo'self, the game is cold, but it's fair."

No other words were necessary.

Don squeezed the trigger and watched the bullet enter the top of Diego's head.

Diego's body swayed back and forth as if deciding in which direction to fall. Finally it toppled over onto its side.

With the back of his hand, Don wiped the blood and gore from his face. Suddenly he became ill from the sickly sweet wine of death. Staggering like he was intoxicated, Don stumbled from the backyard. His pistol was still clutched tightly in his hand. How he made his unsteady legs carry him to where Weed-Eyes should have been parked he would never know. Instead of the invitation of a waiting vehicle to spirit him to safety he found only an empty, uncaring street.

"Damn!" he shouted angrily. "I don't believe this fucking shit!"

Two men had been killed over his cocaine, and the person he trusted the most had still managed to beat him out of his kilo. Tucking his pistol into his waistband he straightened up the best he could and headed for home.

14

NINE MINUTES LATER DON SLIPPED HIS KEY INTO THE
back door of his house. He made sure that he double-locked
the door before cutting through the kitchen and bounding
up the stairs to his room. Juanita was gone. *She must have
went to the store or something,* he thought. He sat on the
bed and decided to wait for her; they could leave the minute
she returned.

While he waited, Don decided to pack a light traveling bag. Only the bare necessities—a few clothes, his
money, crackpipes, and his remaining kilo of cocaine. They
wouldn't need much more than that. Don planned to return
home as soon as the heat died down from the murder he'd
committed. He really wasn't worried about the heat coming
down on him, though. Lonnie had killed Sajak and Don

doubted very seriously that he was going to go to the cops. The only other person that could put two and two together to come up with the fact that he had murdered Diego was Weed-Eyes. Don seriously doubted that Weed-Eyes was around when the fireworks started, so Don wasn't worried about him as a witness. Right now Weed-Eyes was somewhere with a kilo of cocaine and $20,000 in cash. Don had to smile despite how angry he was. He would have done the same thing himself. But that wasn't going to stop him from cooking Weed-Eyes if he bumped into him.

Don threw his mother's striped laundry bag on the bed and began tossing items into it. In the closet he felt around on the shelf for the kilo. Nothing. Quickly he dragged a chair over to the closet and stood on it, peering onto the shelf. As he looked at the empty shelf a feeling of déjà vu washed over him.

Frantically he searched his bedroom, but his search was fruitless. Juanita. The idea of her running off with his kilo sent shivers up his spine.

"Motherfucka!" he shouted at the top of his lungs, pounding his thighs with his clenched fists. "Motherfucking, thieving-ass bitch!"

Don took out his frustration on his bedroom. He overturned the television, threw the stereo on the floor, and dumped his chest of drawers. Next, he flipped the bed and threw his Chicago Bears football-helmet lamp out the window. It thudded into the house next door, then crashed to the ground.

"Don? What's wrong with you?" Rhonda screamed from outside his room.

"Leave me alone, Rhonda!" Don seethed.

"What's going on in there, boy? What the hell is all that noise? Imma call Mama if you don't quit making all that doggone noise!"

"Leave me alone, girl! I'm looking for something!"

"Well you better quit making that noise, I'm trying to sleep!"

"Alright, alright."

When Rhonda left from outside his door, Don sat in the wreckage of his room, in the middle of the floor in the dark, and smoked several large pipe bowls of crack. The more he smoked, the angrier he became. He stuffed his warm pipe into his pocket, loaded his gun, and left the house.

Sunrise was still about five hours away as Don walked aimlessly through the streets. The night was warm and the streets were teeming with nightlife, but any person who crossed Don's path gave the wide-eyed young man a wide berth. The walk began to dissipate the charge he received from his last hit of crack, so he dipped into an alley and took another hit. Recharged, he resumed his search for Weed-Eyes and Juanita.

Desperation began to set in. He had been walking for hours and wasn't any closer to his betrayers. As he walked past an apartment building, he heard the song by the Geto Boys, "My Mind Playin' Tricks on Me." He thought, *yeah my mind is definitely playing tricks on me if I think Imma bump into that green-eyed bastard. Weed-Eyes is long gone,* he concluded. Don knew that no hype in his right mind would stick around with a whole slab of cocaine and twenty thou. Weed-Eyes could have driven to another area code by now.

Don stopped in an alley and sat on some back porch steps to smoke again. Juanita was a different matter, however. She didn't have her own transportation, nor the mental inclination to sell the cocaine. Knowing Juanita, she would probably try to smoke the whole thing. He took another blast and continued to think. He had to find Juanita and recover as much of his cocaine as possible. He knew for a fact that Juanita wouldn't go home to the small apartment she shared with her drunken mother and four brothers—she hated it there. The only other place she might've gone to was Wanda's house on Cottage Grove. She was the only friend Juanita ever seemed to mention. It wasn't so far-fetched for Don to think she'd gone there.

With the ease of a lifelong ghetto dweller, Don picked his way through the alleys and gangways until he reached the projects on Cottage Grove. Two-story walk-ups lined either side of the busy boulevard. He didn't know which apartment Wanda lived in. He described her to a group of young guys standing in one of the parking lots. He didn't know if they bought his story about being Wanda's long-lost cousin, but he accepted their directions.

Outside the apartment door, Don glanced around to make sure no curious neighbors were watching and then he gave the door a well-aimed kick. The flimsy lock buckled under the pressure. Don whipped out his pistol and charged into the apartment like a DEA agent on a drug raid.

In the living room he caught Juanita, Wanda, and Raoul in various stages of a crack party: Raoul had a pipe to his lips, Wanda was on the couch with a razor blade in her hand, and Juanita was cleaning her pipe.

Don's and Juanita's eyes locked on one another. She had a shocked look on her face from Don's sudden appearance. Shock turned to terror as she recalled what Don promised to do to her if she ever stole from him again. The wicked-looking pistol in his hand confirmed his threat.

"He gone kill me!" Juanita screamed hysterically. "He gone kill me!"

Juanita's scream mobilized Raoul, who didn't see the pistol in Don's hand; all he saw was someone trying to fuck up their good time. There was no way Raoul could let that happen—not when Juanita had shown up with more cocaine than he'd ever seen in his life and was setting it out. If Raoul could help it, Don wasn't going to lay one hand on Juanita.

Raoul dropped his pipe, jumped to his feet, and charged, brandishing an end table he'd scooped up, all the while screaming.

Don silenced him by shooting Raoul in the left knee. Raoul flipped over the sofa, smashing himself in the face with the end table.

Wanda watched Raoul get shot before she silently exploded into action. Moving swiftly and silently, Wanda slashed Don's forearm with the razor blade in her hand before he could react.

Don tried to fend her off without shooting her, but received several more slashes on his arms. He backpedaled and stumbled over one of the children's toys, but recovered in time to dodge a razor slash aimed at his throat. With his free hand he snatched a heavy ashtray from the dinette table and smashed it against Wanda's temple. The force from the blow knocked all the fight from Wanda and she fell to the floor with an ugly gash alongside her right eye.

Juanita knew Don was coming for her next and before he could take one step in her direction, she leaped from her seat, grabbed the kilo, and jumped out the window. Don stood with his mouth hanging open until he remembered they were only on the second floor. He made his way over to the window prepared to follow her example. On his way across the living room Wanda grabbed his leg in a feeble attempt to restrain him.

Don aimed a vicious kick at her face, but her hold on his leg threw him off balance and he landed hard on his butt.

Now Don was salty.

Untangling himself enough to get on his feet, Don squeezed the trigger of his .357 and ventilated Wanda's stretch-mark-covered stomach with a dime-sized hole.

Wanda released Don's leg and began screaming while she clutched her abdomen.

Ignoring Wanda's howls, Don continued over to the window and prepared to jump. He remembered to look before he leaped. Placing his hands on the windowsill, he peered out into the night.

Juanita had made the second-story drop without incurring any serious injury—only bruising her butt from an awkward landing. She had taken a moment to make sure no bones were broken, but the sound of Don shooting Wanda in the apartment made her vault to her feet. She was so paranoid from smoking yams she believed Don was shooting at her. Like an Olympic sprinter, she kicked up her heels and ran into the street.

Cottage Grove has always been one of the busiest boulevards on Chicago's South Side and the early morning hour was no exception. Juanita was so scared for her life she ran into the street, paying no heed to the oncoming traffic.

Juanita never saw the headlights or heard the protesting squeal of the tires before a speeding flatbed tow truck slammed into her. The grille of the truck struck her high in the chest. Her head whipped back with a grisly snap before she somersaulted thirty feet into the air. Juanita was dead before her body landed and slid to a stop half a block from the initial impact.

Even in death Juanita refused to let go of the cocaine. The kilo had accompanied Juanita during her airborne somersaults, but it burst when she slammed into the asphalt. A miniature mushroom cloud of cocaine erupted, covering the immediate area with a powdery layer of the controlled substance.

From Wanda's apartment window, Don watched Juanita's

grisly death with a mixture of emotions. He felt a slight twinge of guilt for the part he played in her demise, and anger from witnessing his beautiful cocaine spread all over the street where it was no use to anyone.

Disgusted, Don turned from the window and walked over to take a seat on the urine-smelling couch. Not paying the slightest bit of attention to the two wounded cluckers, Don picked up a crackpipe. He took a chunk of crack from the mirror on the coffee table and dropped it on the screen in the pipe bowl. After melting the crack with one of the numerous torches on the table, Don put his lips to the stem and sucked the smoke into his nervous system.

When Don stood up, his head was reeling from taking such a gigantic hit. His heart was beating hard in his chest. He managed to steady himself, then swept the crack off the mirror into the bag he was carrying in his pocket. As he headed for the door, a devious thought entered his haze-shrouded mind. On the dinette table was a bottle of rubbing alcohol that Wanda and Raoul used to rub on their mosquito bites, a side effect of sleeping in an apartment without screens on the window. With a wicked grin on his face Don poured the contents on the ragged furniture. He threw the empty bottle on the floor. He packed his pipe again from the plastic bag and lit a torch. He held the torch to the bowl and took another godfather hit. As he walked toward the door he exhaled the smoke. On the threshold he turned and tossed the flaming torch onto an alcohol-drenched easy chair.

Instantly the chair ignited. Quickly the fire spread to the sofa and that was all she wrote.

Not concerned in the slightest about Wanda's and Raoul's welfare or that of her children, Don slammed the door as he left the apartment.

Raoul rescued all but two of the children with the help of the neighbors. The early morning news carried accounts of the accidental death of an eighteen-year-old girl carrying a large amount of cocaine. They would also milk the topics of the two children murdered in a fire set by an unknown arsonist.

Detective Carson and Detective Winters were assigned to the case and interviewed the bedridden witnesses at the hospital. The two detectives pieced together a shaky story from Wanda, who was in critical but stable condition with burns on 40 percent of her body and a bullet wound in her stomach.

The culprit the detectives would come to know as Donald Haskill, alias Don-Don or Don, had vanished into the night. Neither detective knew it, but they would hear that name again and again. When they finally got a chance to interview the boy brought in earlier that night suffering from a gunshot wound, he would blame Don also.

When the detectives left Wanda's room, she received more visitors. Four distraught young men wanted to know why their baby sister was in a steel drawer in the morgue.

One of the men, father of one of Wanda's dead children, wanted to know if the same culprit was responsible for the death of his son, too.

Recognizing her opportunity for revenge, Wanda lied to the four brothers about Juanita's death. She told them Don pushed Juanita in front of the truck and that he purposely burned up two of Wanda's sons.

The brothers left in a hurry.

In the meantime, Don sat alone in his room at home smoking crack. He heard someone banging on the door and a voice called out, "Open up, it's the police!" By the time his sister got up to let them in, he had escaped out the window and was a block away.

Rhonda opened the door to see what the police wanted and they pushed past her. "Hold on. You can't come in like this. My mother is a policewoman. I know my rights. What's this about?"

"We're looking for somebody and we have information that he lives here," Detective Carson said gruffly as he moved into the living room.

"Where's your warrant?" Rhonda asked defiantly.

Carson scowled. "We don't need one if we have reason to believe that a suspect fleeing from a crime ran into this residence."

"Nobody has fled anywhere. What are you talking about? This don't sound right. I'm calling my mother."

Detective Winters grabbed Rhonda's arm softly but firmly. "Does Donald Haskill live here?"

"Yes, that my little brother. He isn't here. What you want with him?"

"We just have a couple of questions for him," Detective Winters said as she nodded her head to two uniformed officers.

Guns drawn, the two policemen headed up the carpeted steps.

"Where the hell are they going?" Rhonda asked. "I told you that my brother wasn't here."

"But he does live here?" Detective Carson said from over by the mantelpiece. "This him in this photo?"

The picture was of Don on his sixteenth birthday, taken on the front porch.

"Yes, that's him. You still haven't told me what this is all about, though."

Just then the two cops came down the stairs.

"Anything?" Carson asked.

"Nothing," one of the officers answered. "We found what had to be his room. It's in a shambles. Window was open leading out onto the back porch roof. Looks like our guy left in a hurry."

Winters pulled a business card from her pocket and handed it to Rhonda. "If your brother comes home, give him our card and make sure he gives us a call. Tell him that since your mother is on the job, he doesn't have to worry about being mistreated. Let's go."

Rhonda noticed Carson trying to slide the photograph of

Don in his pocket. "What are you doing! I didn't say that you could take that."

Carson's face turned slightly red. "Well, we need this to identify a suspect in an ongoing investigation and . . ."

Winters cut in. "Do you mind very much if we take the picture? We'll do our best to get it back to you."

"I guess so. Don't hurt my brother. I don't know what he's supposed to have done, but don't hurt him."

"We won't," Winters assured her as she swept the uniformed officers and her partner out the door. "He'll be okay. Good night and sorry to bother you."

While the police were leaving his mother's house, the only thing Don cared about was making it to the little, seedy motel on King Drive. There he could rent a room and lay low. As long as he had crack and money he was straight.

THE COBWEBS AND MURKINESS CLEARED AS LONNIE
awoke with a gasp. He plummeted back into the limbo of
his partial coma. Before he went under he heard an authoritative voice summon the doctor.

Three hours later Lonnie awakened for the second time.
A million needles of pain stabbed him as he debated whether
to open his eyes. Several excruciating attempts resulted in
failure. Finally he gave up, content to stare at the inside of
his eyelids.

It was no minor miracle Lonnie was still alive. When the
burning slug from Don's pistol burrowed into his flesh it felt
like his soul was on fire. Scared that Don was still on his
trail, he had cut through a gangway and ran into a backyard. Big mistake. In the dark he had nearly split his skull on

the porch as he rounded the small house. Slamming into the ancient wood of the porch had knocked the wind and almost the life out of him. Scarlet blood pumped out of the gash in his forehead and the hole in his stomach. All he could remember was a voice from deep down inside telling him to get up. He tried to ignore the voice, but it was persistent. Marshaling all his strength he somehow maneuvered onto his hands and knees and began to crawl through the gangway that led to the street. The ninety feet of pavement he spanned seemed like ninety miles. Several times he blacked out from losing such a large amount of blood. Finally he made it to the street and flagged down a motorist.

The motorist summoned emergency assistance via his cell phone. Police and an ambulance arrived in a relatively short time. At Cook County hospital the doctors worked for seven hours to stabilize Lonnie. From there he was moved to intensive care. He was in a drug-induced coma for three days before he regained consciousness for the first time.

He pretended to be unconscious while he listened for several hours to the doctors and police detectives. Lonnie learned the detectives hoped he would recover so they could question him about Sajak's and Diego's murders. Detectives Winters and Carson had gone over the crime scene with a fine-tooth comb. Their guess was Lonnie was the only survivor of a drug deal gone bad. That was why they were sitting on Lonnie, waiting for any improvement in his condition. It was so rare to find a living witness when drug deals went bad. If Lonnie regained consciousness and could tell them who was responsible for the carnage in the backyard it would be an easy case.

Detective Arnold Carson was a portly, middle-aged white man of average height. He was raised by hardworking, poor parents in Burbank. He never liked Blacks until he had a chance to meet some of them and work with them. He never considered himself bigoted, but his partner, Detective Almeta Winters, a Black woman, had helped him over the years to dispel his prejudicial tendencies.

Almeta Winters was a horse of a different color—an eternal optimist and perennial do-gooder. The soft-spoken, dark-skinned woman was tough, cunning, and fair. Her skill at interrogation was renowned in their division, whereas Carson would resort to brutal methods to obtain confessions and information. Together they made a dynamite team of homicide detectives. The differences in their techniques complemented instead of hindered one another.

Lonnie listened to the detectives talk until he fell asleep. When he woke again he felt stronger than before, but he was still in quite a bit of pain. Gathering up all his courage he opened his eyes. He wiggled his fingers and toes to make sure he could feel them.

Neither detective noticed Lonnie's movements. Carson was engrossed in a game of solitaire and Winters was staring out of the window, daydreaming about her upcoming vacation. The sound of Lonnie's voice surprised both of them.

"What a nigga got to do to get a cup of water in this

motherfucka?" Lonnie rasped. His tongue felt swollen and sluggish in his mouth.

Carson jumped to his feet, knocking over the small table he had been playing cards on, and rushed over to Lonnie's bedside. "I'm Detective Carson and I need to ask you a few questions, boy."

"First thing you need to know is that boys run from the age of one to twelve," Lonnie said. "Second, I don't give a fuck if you was Commissioner Gordon, I ain't got shit to say to the police. Now like I said before, I want a cup of water."

Carson laughed at Lonnie's sarcasm. He toyed with the teen's IV as he said smoothly, "I bet you think you sounded tough saying that, little punk. They told me you was crying like a baby when they brought you in here. That's okay though, we won't tell any of your gangster friends that you shitted your pants when you got shot in the stomach."

Detective Winters stood quietly by the window and watched. "Detective, can I see you out in the hallway for a minute?"

"Sure, no problem. Make sure you don't go nowhere; we'll be back."

In the hallway they walked down by the elevators because the nurses' station was close to Lonnie's door.

Winters asked, "How you want to crack this egg?"

"I don't care," Carson said with a bored expression on his face. "It really don't even make a difference."

"How 'bout a little good cop, bad cop?"

"No way, Winters. You always get to play the good cop

and I've got to come off like the racist bastard every time. Not this time. It's my turn to play good cop."

Winters twisted her lips.

"What, you don't think I can play good cop? I've got a good-cop routine. You just never give me a chance to use it. Remember the little girl that was killing johns? I went in there with my good cop and she told me all about killing those two tricks for their wallets. My good-cop routine got that confession."

"Man, that don't even count. You didn't have to do nothing on that one but be white. That inbred daughter of a Ku Klux Klan sharecropper didn't want to talk to me 'cause I'm Black. That didn't have nothing to do with your good-cop routine. I've seen you use it before and it's lacking at best. Just face it, I'm the good cop and you're the evil white devil."

"Yeah, whatever, sister girl. I'm going to get me some coffee."

"Don't put too much cream in it, Nazi."

Carson laughed as he punched the button for the elevator. "Sounds like you want this cream in your coffee."

"You got to be kidding me," Winters laughed.

Carson stepped onto the elevator. Winters replaced her grin with a kind, concerned look. She entered Lonnie's room and pretended to ignore the belligerent boy. She righted the card table and gathered the deck of cards from the floor. She shuffled them and dealt herself a hand of solitaire.

Lonnie couldn't take the silent treatment.

"What the fuck you want, Miss Piggy?"

Winters placed a red six on a black seven. "Don't pay me no attention. I won't bother you. I know that you're in a lot of pain."

"This ain't shit," Lonnie said bravely. "This little shit ain't gone stop me. Where did yo honkey-ass partner go?"

Winters continued her card game. "He went to get some coffee. He hasn't had much sleep in the last few days, you know. Plus he's a little uptight. You would be too if you hadn't had pussy since pussy had you."

Her witticism sponsored a throaty laugh from Lonnie that triggered a coughing fit. Winters jumped up and poured him a glass of water from the bedside pitcher and helped him drink it.

Lonnie wouldn't say it, but he was grateful for her act of kindness. He had already decided that for a cop she wasn't half bad. He could see that she was really pretty in an understated way and her brownish-black hair had to hang to the middle of her back even though it was swept up in a neat ponytail. Plus she had a body. Even with her blazer on, he could see that she had some nice breasts and her blue jeans hugged her butt.

Sensing she had his full attention, Winters returned to her seat and dealt herself another hand of solitaire. Lonnie thought she had forgotten about him when she said, "Lonnie, I just want to help you."

"How you gone help me, cop?" Lonnie growled, trying to maintain his tough-guy act.

"I just want to know who killed your friends and shot you. I know that by the code of the streets you guys don't like to talk to the police, but I swear it's different this time. This guy doesn't deserve your silence. Not for what he did to your friends and to you. By you remaining silent all you're managing to do is protect this guy from what he's got coming to him. It doesn't make sense for you to protect this guy."

"You don't give a fuck about me or my homies, so I wish you would stop acting, cop. This shit is yo job! We live this shit every day! It's our lives! Now you sitting up in here acting like the white man's justice is gone do my homies a bit of good. Bullshit! Fuck the white man's justice! The best way is street justice. You and that cracker partner of yours ain't finta get no promotion off my nigga's blood."

Winters acknowledged Lonnie's remarks by nodding her head. She dealt herself another hand of solitaire. This kid was turning out to be a little deeper than she had gauged. She decided to try another angle. She still hadn't used her secret weapon. She hated to use it, but this thing needed to be wrapped up so the lieutenant would get off their backs and she could pack for Aruba.

She continued to play solitaire. "Okay, Lonnie, let me put it in the raw for you. You got bigger problems than this little shit. You and all the rest of them hustling over at Harper Court are about to be indicted. You geniuses and entrepreneurs have been serving drugs to the feds for the last eighteen months. The feds, baby. Y'all aren't going to be at the courts down at 26th and California Hirkoon building. Federal court all the way. They don't even give you your time in years. They give you your sentence in months. You're going to have to go back to your cell and get a piece of paper and a pencil to figure out just how much time they gave you.

"Y'all have been out there serving that shit like it was legal. I must admit it was a good operation, but you boys forgot that you were less than a thousand feet from a school. Tsk, tsk. I've seen the paperwork on this one. They are going to lose you guys in the system—the whole crew. That is except for the big mouths that they've already flipped. Yeah, that's right. It's amazing just how much the thuggiest nigga will tell when he faced with all that time. A thousand months at least is a guarantee on this one. Your boss Diego is lucky he got killed. They were going after him on a kingpin beef. That means they could execute him. The rest of you guys they just wanted to park for the rest of your natural life."

Suddenly Lonnie felt sick and it didn't have anything to do with his bullet wound.

Without looking up from her game, Winters moved in for the kill. "Now before you start talking that innocent shit, think about this. You need me. I can make this thing with the feds go away. And I'm the only one that can do it. But you've got to scratch my back before I can scratch yours. If I get the name of the shooter, the feds will forget they ever heard of you. If I don't, you can look forward to life in the fed pen. But we can avoid all that if you give me a name and run down the whole scene to me. You can't incriminate yourself because we need you to testify against this asshole."

Lonnie was sweating. Everything Detective Winters said dropped on him like an anvil. Drug indictments of the sort she mentioned were numerous in the ghetto, but he never thought he would see the day his name was on one of those lists. It was a given he didn't want to sit in the joint for the rest of his days. The choices she gave him really weren't choices at all; no matter how cleverly she disguised them, they were ultimatums.

"I'll tell you whatever you want," Lonnie conceded, sensing this was one jam he couldn't bluff his way out of. "I'll give you this stud's name, but you got to hold me down. I know all about this cat—where he lay his head and all that. Just give me a minute to think this shit over."

"Okay," Winters said, adjusting the straps of her shoulder holster as she left the room. It was all she could do to hide her smile of triumph.

If Lonnie would have seen the smile on her lips, his ghetto instinct could have warned him against trusting her. It didn't take long for him to mull over the situation. He really didn't have any alternative but to tell her the truth.

"Detective Winters!" he called out in a slightly, shaky voice.

Winters peeked into the room. "You ready to let me know something? Or are you still wasting my time?"

"Is you sure the feds gone forget about me?" Lonnie asked.

Winters stepped into the room and shut the door. "As sure as my asshole points toward the ground."

"Alright, the nigga name is Donald Haskill. They call him Don-Don or Don. He stay over on 64th and Langley. The house number is 6417."

Winters pulled a small notebook and pen out of her pocket and flipped it open. "I got the name. How's about a description?"

"He 'bout six feet, I think. Caramel complexion. No real face hair with short, wavy hair on his head. I'd say the nigga wear about 160 pounds."

"That's good enough. Now tell me what happened in that backyard and don't lie. We already know that it was drug related."

Lonnie took a sip of water. "The shit went down like this. Don called Diego and told my man he had a slab of some good shit for sale. We checked it out and the shit was super-tight, so we agreed to buy it for twenty gees. He told us to meet him at the building at twelve that night and bring the scratch. When we got there it looked like everything was straight. We made the buy and we was about to leave when Don grabbed Sajak and blew his brains out. Next he shot me in the stomach, then I guess he killed Diego."

"You're lying," Winters said, her voice barely above a whisper.

"Huh?"

"I said you're lying. First off, we found a shotgun with Sajak's prints all over it in the garage. It hadn't been fired. The slug that we dug out of Diego and the one out of your stomach didn't match the one from Sajak. We found your gun with your prints and blood all over it. Also there was gunpowder residue on your hands. We know that either you or Diego shot Sajak. From what we could patch together it looks like you guys tried to rob this kid. All the time, you smart guys underestimated him." Detective Winters stood, buttoned her blazer, and headed for the door. "Thanks for your cooperation. We'll be in touch."

"That's all!" Lonnie shouted. "I spill my motherfucking guts and that's all! How I'm gone know if you cleared my damn name! Come back here! This shit ain't right!"

His words fell on deaf ears. As Winters walked to the elevator she could still hear Lonnie ranting and raving. In the cafeteria she purchased a cup of coffee and sat with her partner.

Carson folded the *Tribune* he had been reading and waited for his partner to speak.

Winters blew on the cup of steaming coffee. "Hold on to your shirt. The kid we're looking for about that fire is really popular. Lonnie says that Don shot him and killed our two victims. We know that's a lie. The kid had to be the one that did Diego, though. Little asshole is up there lying his ass off."

"Shit!" Carson exclaimed. "One kid did all that in one night. He was pretty busy. There must have been some serious money involved."

"Yeah, twenty thousand and a kilo of coke. It was the kid's coke. From Lonnie's story and the way it was laid out, they tried to rob the kid and he outsmarted them. He must have had some help, but Lonnie didn't mention it. Don't forget about the girl that was hit by the truck by the house fire. It was coke all over the ground. Not enough to get much of anything for the lab, but the wrapping let us know it had to be a kilo. I'm thinking that the girl had his drugs too. She gets chased out into traffic by him. He's trying to get his drugs or kill her or both. Tow truck hits her, that's the end of that kilo. I don't think it was the same kilo that they tried to rob him for. I think it was another kilo. That makes two kilos. Two kilos, twenty-thousand bucks, and Don-Don. I can see why this kid was on the warpath. It looks like he was being crossed out of his drugs from all sides."

Carson shook his head. "You had to do something special to get that out of the kid. What did you do, promise the little punk your hand in marriage?"

"It didn't take all that. I simply told the little punk about the feds' case against him and his friends. I told him I could get his name off the feds' list."

Carson looked confused. "What case are you talking about?"

"The one I made up."

"And he fell for that shit?" Carson asked, chuckling heartily. "Damn, Winters, I'm proud of you. You're getting downright sneaky."

Winters took another sip of the scalding, sugary coffee. "The poor bastard thought I could get him off a federal drug beef. He wasn't even smart enough to realize that homicide can't stop an ongoing federal narcotics investigation. I had to make it sound real convincing so this fish would jump into my boat. And you can keep your little smart-ass remarks about me marrying beneath me. You know I'm saving myself for you, big fella."

Carson laughed at his partner's Mae West impression.

"Sorry you had to miss my evil-cop routine."

"Evil-cop routine?"

"That's like the advanced version of the bad-cop routine. It's not for amateurs like you. You have to give yourself over to the dark side. The only problem is inexperienced guys like you can't make it back."

"Get the hell out of here. What next?"

As she blew on her cup of coffee, Winters said, "I was thinking that we should go see if the ballistics have come back on the gun we found with Lonnie's prints. If I'm right his gun is the one that killed Sajak, and if I'm right you owe me dinner. And I'm not talking about Budweisers and pretzels. I want a real dinner. Something with meat and vegetables."

"Why you always got to treat me like I'm a redneck?"

" 'Cause you know you got some redneck in you. I

would have offered to let you have me for dinner, but I know you don't eat dark meat."

They laughed all the way to their unmarked Ford. Carson was still laughing as he pulled out of the parking lot, showing the attendant his badge in lieu of money. As they left, a black Toyota 4Runner pulled into the parking lot.

Three young men emerged from the vehicle. Timberland boots and AirJordan shoes adorned their feet and their expensive jewelry was displayed for all to see. They walked into the hospital and headed straight for the elevators.

On the seventh floor the three boys entered Lonnie's room. One of the boys locked the door while the other two approached the bed. The short, dark leader of the boys swept his dreadlocks out of his face and pulled a 9-millimeter from under his jean jacket. Holding the pistol sideways, he tapped Lonnie's forehead with the tempered steel of the barrel.

Lonnie opened his eyes and winced at the sight of the pistol to his head.

"Let me introduce myself," the boy with the gun said. "I'm Domino of the East Side Apostles. These two niggas here is my rappees. This right here in my hand is a Taurus. I know that may sound cliché, but it's actually a real nice pistol. And you know what they say 'bout fucking with the bull and you get the horns. Now if you don't want to tell me who killed my cousin, Imma make you lose yo memory permanently."

"Who-who is y-y-yo cousin?" Lonnie stuttered.

"Nigga, Sajak was my motherfuckin' cousin! First cousin."

"I didn't know that man. I'm sorry 'bout that shit. Sh-sh-shorty was a good little homie."

Domino emphasized his words by putting the pistol barrel in Lonnie's ear. "Nigga, save the drama fo yo mama. I don't want to hear that shit. I ain't here to hear about his sterling personal qualities. I came here to find out who killed my family, stud. If I have to ask you again it's gone be one less bullet in this motherfucking heater."

Lonnie rapid-fired, "The nigga name is Don. He live on 64th and Langley. He got a girlfriend named Juanita."

Satisfied that Lonnie was too scared to lie, Domino took the pistol from Lonnie's head and stuck it back inside his jacket. He nodded to his homie to unlock the door and they left Lonnie in bad need of a bedpan.

In the hospital parking lot, Domino climbed behind the wheel of his SUV and waited for his boys to get in. The moment their respective doors slammed closed he threw the truck into gear and sped to the attendant's booth. Disregarding the price of his parking stub, Domino threw a twenty-dollar bill into the attendant's face and swerved under the parking-lot stick. Tears trickled from Domino's eyes and wove their way down his face.

"Listen up, niggas!" Domino barked. "We gone find this stud that killed my baby cousin. I personally want to off this punk. We gone squeeze these motherfucking streets until somebody give this nigga up. He got to die for killing one of mine."

Both boys knew Domino was deadly serious. There would be hell to pay for killing a family member of an Apostle. The price was blood; innocent or otherwise really didn't matter.

DON WAS GOING STIR-CRAZY. HE HAD BEEN COOPED UP IN the motel room for five days, leaving only to go to the vending machines and to pay the manager every day. The maid that came to clean the room was becoming suspicious about a young boy holed up for so long. While she was making the bed and emptying the garbage cans she would sneak glances at Don as he watched television or slept. Whatever her suspicions were she must have spoken to the manager because he tried to enter Don's room using the passkey. The security chain was the only thing that stopped him and he sputtered and stuttered when Don questioned his motives.

The damage was done, though—the manager had gotten a good look at his face. Spooked, Don checked out. He had nowhere to go, plus he craved female companionship. He had to admit that he was getting lonely and bored.

He hoped that some of the heat on the streets had died down. Maybe not much, but enough for it to be reasonably safe to find a woman and another room. Small, cheap motels were plentiful in this neighborhood, if not he could take a chance and venture farther south past 79th on Stony Island. There were a million cheap motels lining the huge boulevard there, so that wouldn't be a problem. Right now he wanted a decent-looking girl. She could even be a crackhead if she wasn't too far gone. Crack would definitely give them a common thread and she wouldn't ask too many questions if he let her get as high as she wanted.

It was close to dusk and Don walked briskly down the streets looking over his shoulder every few steps. His pistol felt heavy in the waistband of his pants. In his back pocket he could hear the jiggling sound of extra rounds of ammunition. First he had to think where he could find a girl. He had decided it would be pushing his luck to look for a woman on 63rd Street. He had been hanging out on that street for most of his young life and he was just too well known for that. He decided his best bet would be the Ida B. Wells projects.

He knew from experience that the girls there didn't have a lot of the inhibitions regular city girls might. In the Wells, sex was a trading commodity instead of an act of love. It wouldn't prove too hard for him to find a willing prospect there.

Don hopped on the bus, which deposited him on the southwest corner of the Wells. The Wells looked deceptively peaceful to blissfully ignorant tourists, but veterans of Chicago's streets knew it was one of the most infamous housing projects in the city. It had seen its share of notoriously rich drug dealers, murderous street gangs, and people capable of behavior that society classified as immoral.

Life was cheap here. Don had been to the Wells many times and it never ceased to amaze him just how wild it was. Drug peddlers shamelessly hawked their wares in hallways. Scantily clad females fought, cursed, and drank on the stoops and corners. Young gang members roamed in bloodthirsty packs ready to defend their homeland at the sound of a shot. Their street-warped minds couldn't comprehend life outside of the Wells or growing old.

Don was a youthful veteran of the streets, so it was a simple matter for him to blend in with his surroundings. He ignored the drug dealers trying to get his attention. He ignored the crackhead and dope-fiend hoes as they called and whistled at him. Don knew they wouldn't hesitate to slit his throat for ten dollars.

The prostitutes rained insults on him when they saw he wasn't shopping. To get away from them, Don ducked around a corner and bumped into a tall, slim, pock-faced man. Don tried to apologize and continue on his way, but the man grabbed his arm.

"Hey, motherfucka!" the man said. "Pussy-ass nigga, you stepped on my goddamn shoe!"

Don looked the tall man up and down. He was dressed in an expensive-looking suit and wore a beautiful pair of dress shoes. The dull glow and dark spots in the man's face alerted Don he was a dope fiend. Don knew he didn't need any trouble so he tried to back down gracefully.

"My fault, my man," Don said apologetically. "I ain't mean to step on yo shoes and shit, but you ain't got to be calling me all out my name."

The tall dope fiend bent over and wiped his shoes. "Little pussy-ass nigga, I'm 'bout to go play for some major paper and yo ho ass done fucked up the shine on my damn shoes. I should slap the shit out yo bitch . . ."

That was all the dope fiend managed to say. Quickly, Don stepped close to him before he could stand up and rocketed a nasty uppercut into the dope fiend's jaw. Don followed the uppercut with a left hook that put the man on his ass. He thought the man was down for the count.

Holding his nose, the man fished a hunting knife with a serrated blade out of his sock. Rocking all the while, he climbed to his feet. "You young-ass street punk, you got problems now. I'm 'bout to put you where yo mama can't kiss you and yo loved ones gone miss you."

Don backpedaled in barely enough time to prevent himself from being gutted like a fish. His hands were sweating as he pulled his pistol from his waistband.

"Bitch nigga," the dope fiend said, as he advanced on Don. "You think 'cause you got a missile I'm sposed to be scared. You better use it, bitch!"

Smiling, Don shot the man in his left thigh.

As he fell to the ground, Don heard someone call out, "That's what yo dope-fiend ass get, Cannon Charlie!"

Someone else joined in. "Yeah, nigga! You always trying to bully some shorty! Shorty right there done put a hole in you ass!"

To the people of the Wells, violence was an everyday way of life—something to break up the monotony and boredom. None of the witnesses of the shooting blamed Don or even cared enough to call the paramedics or police.

Don left the dope fiend on the ground howling and holding his thigh. Two blocks away he found what he thought he was looking for in a companion. As he stopped to remove the spent shell from his burner, he looked up and saw a fine young girl standing on the porch of one of the Wells' numerous apartments. She couldn't have been more than sixteen or seventeen. She looked like a beautiful slice of chocolate cake. Mini-micro braids were piled into a ponytail on her head. A skintight pair of jeans hugged her lower curves while a baby T-shirt smothered her upper curves. Every detail of her body, from her pouting glossed lips to her shapely thighs, screamed sex.

Before he could take one step toward her a flaming red Monte Carlo whipped into the parking space in front of the girl's porch. A short, yellow man hopped out of the car, ran around it, and ran up to the girl. The look of fear on the girl's face let Don know this was someone she wasn't happy to see. Harshly, the man grabbed the girl's arm and began shouting in her face. She was a few inches taller than the man so the scene looked comical. She tried to pull away and he slapped her face.

The girl burst into tears.

The man tried to herd her into his car; she resisted and received another slap for her troubles.

Don had seen enough. He didn't care who the yellow nigga was to her. Don knew he had to have this girl. He crossed the street at a brisk pace and got right in the middle of the fray.

The little man tried to slap the girl again, but Don grabbed his wrist and held it firmly in a vise-like grip. Don's actions stunned the short fellow—this newcomer was out of pocket.

"Nigga, who the fuck is you?" the short man screeched as he tried to free himself from Don's grip.

"I'm Don-Don, nigga. Who the fuck is you?"

"Shorty Rob, fool! Nigga, I don't even know you. Why the fuck you got yo nose in my fucking business?"

Before Don answered, he took his first close look at the girl Shorty Rob had been slapping around. He thought she looked good from across the street, but up close, she looked like a beauty queen. She stopped crying and curiously looked her Samaritan up and down. Obviously she liked what she saw because she smiled at Don.

That was all Don needed to see. Shorty Rob was just a minor obstacle in his path. As good as this girl looked, Don would slay Shorty Rob right here if need be.

Don ignored Shorty Rob still struggling in his grasp. "Baby girl, what's yo name? And is this yo man?"

"Yeah, that's my girl," Shorty Rob answered.

He received a chilling glance from Don.

"My name is Rena," the girl said. "And this sorry-ass nigga used to be my man. That is until I caught him giving my friend a rim job in my fucking house. Now he mad 'cause I don't want to fuck with him no more. Shit-breath nigga."

"So now the nigga want to come round and gorilla you, huh?" Don asked, looking at Shorty Rob.

"Nall, it ain't like that," Shorty Rob explained. "I just done invested a lot of time and money in this young bitch and now she trying to front on me."

Shorty Rob was playing for time. It had just dawned on him that the name Don-Don sounded familiar. This was the nigga everybody was trying to get their hands on. The East Side Apostles had a nice reward out for anybody that could help them find this boy. The police were also looking for him as a suspect in a multiple homicide. Now that Shorty Rob took a good look at the boy holding his arm, Don did have the eyes of a killer—cold, dark, and soulless. A glance at Don's waist let Rob know he was packing heat. Whatever Shorty Rob may have been, he wasn't a fool; he knew better than to tangle with a ghetto killer.

Don was so preoccupied with Rena he almost forgot he was still holding Shorty Rob's wrist. All the fight seemed to be gone from the little man so he released his grip. If the little nigga wanted to walk away like a player that was cool, but if he wanted to act crazy Don had no qualms about hurting him.

"So Rena, what's up, boo?" Don asked.

"Fuck that nigga, Don-Don. I'm with you."

"You heard her, player, beat it," Don said smoothly to Shorty Rob.

Shorty Rob held his breath and kept his hands in clear view until he was behind the steering wheel of his car.

Don watched the Monte Carlo until it turned the corner and was out of sight. He slid his arm around Rena's waist and let his hand rest on her ass.

"You get right down to business, don't you?" Rena asked.

"I ain't got no time to be bullshitting. Girl, you need a nigga that take care of his business, not some booty-licking-ass nigga. Rena, what you like to do?"

"What you mean?"

"I mean how you like to kick it? Or in other words, how can a nigga get them tight jeans off you?"

Rena looked at Don with surprise on her face. He could tell she wasn't used to the straightforward approach, but she seemed to like it.

"Well, I don't know if it will get my jeans off, but I do like to smoke me a little weed, drink some Erk & Jerk, and chill."

"Yo wish is my command. But you probably already

know I ain't from around here so I don't know where to get the weed. I can get the E&J from the liquor store up on 39th, though."

"Don't worry about it. I'll send my girl to the store, but she gone want a beer."

"That's cool."

Rena walked into the building and knocked on an apartment door to the right of the staircase. A moment later a woman stuck her head out of the door. Rena explained the mission and the lady was dressed and had her hand out for the money in a minute and thirty seconds.

They watched her walk away.

"We gone stay down here so I can listen for her baby."

"That's cool," Don said.

They exchanged small talk while they waited for Rena's neighbor to return with the weed and alcohol. Ten minutes later, Rena's friend walked up, sat a paper bag on Rena's lap, slipped her beer out of the bag, and disappeared into her apartment.

"C'mon," Rena said.

Don followed her up the stairs and into her apartment. Inside the apartment Don took a seat on the couch and looked around; it was a cozy, clean, little place. The gun in his waistband was uncomfortable in a sitting position. Don took the hand cannon out and set it on the end table. Rena didn't flinch when she saw the pistol.

He looked over at her. "Girl, don't be acting all shy. Roll you some weed up and pour yourself a drink."

Don took a swig of the E&J brandy. "Who live here with you?"

She sat on the couch and took the brandy and poured herself a drink. "Nobody. Just me all by my lonesome. I split my mama's lease with the housing authority to get my own apartment. I been on my own for about nine months. I just started being able to keep my brothers and sisters out of here. Well, really they stopped coming down here 'cause they hated Shorty Rob."

"What was up with that nigga? He was sprung over you wadn't he?"

Rena began rolling up her weed. "Shorty Rob full of shit. I already didn't mind that he had a woman. An old, ugly woman at that. He spent a few dollars on me buying clothes and furniture and think he own me. I didn't ask him for a thing. He went out and spent his money trying to impress me. Then I come home early from work one day because I wasn't feeling good and he had my girl up in here."

Don took another sip of the brandy, letting it burn its way to his stomach. "He was really up in here giving yo girl a rim job."

"Tossing her salad like he had a license. I couldn't believe that shit. I wasn't even mad at her—well, I was, but only because she was up in my house. She's always been a ho so she wasn't out of character. He was totally bogus, though. Up in my house, uhhh."

Rena shivered as she completed her joint.

Don handed her the E&J. "You sound like you need another shot. Yeah, I bet dude is messed up in the head 'bout losing a fine-looking girl like you to me."

"To you?" Rena asked. "I ain't said that I was yours."

"You ain't have to. I could tell that you was gone be mine the minute I saw you."

"Oh yeah?"

"Yeah. I mean we can take it slow, but it's gonna happen anyway so who are we to stand in the way of destiny?"

Rena laughed as she lit the weed. "Boy, you crazy. I like you, Don-Don. You ain't from around here, are you?"

"If I say no, is that a good thing or bad thing?"

"Definitely a good thing. I don't mess with boys from the hood. I grew up with a lot of them, and besides that, when you hit them off with a little something in the bedroom, they like to run around and put your business in the street."

"Well, I'm from over east," Don lied. "I needed a change of scenery from my hood and I was looking for you."

"You was looking for me?" Rena asked as she kicked off her shoes and leaned her head on the back of the couch. She let the weed smoke curl around her head. "How was you looking for me and you just met me?"

"Well, I knew that I was looking for someone that was pretty, cool, and might need my help, and you fit the bill."

"You got game, Don-Don. Look at me, I'm being greedy. You want to hit this?"

"Nall, I don't smoke weed. I smoke crack," Don said.

Rena choked on the weed smoke. "What you say?"

"I smoke crack," Don said plainly. "Is that a problem?"

Rena thought about it a moment. "Not really. I just ain't going to smoke any. It ain't like I ain't never been around it. It's all through here. It seem like everybody use something around here. Either it's coke, dope, weed, or alcohol. Who am I to judge anyway? If that's how you get down, then get down then. Just like I said, though, I don't want any."

They continued to chat as Rena smoked her weed and Don took hits off the pipe.

"Please tell me you got some music over there," Don said, pointing his crackpipe at Rena's small sound system sitting on a bookshelf.

"I got jams, boy," Rena boasted as she walked over to the radio and pushed the power button. "What you want to hear?"

"You got some Tupac, MC Breed, or Ice Cube?"

"Got all that. Well, whatever didn't manage to find its way into my little brother's pockets."

Soon the sounds of Tupac Shakur played softly in the background. When Rena rejoined him on the couch, Don pulled her onto his lap.

"Shorty, I kinda like yo style," Don said.

Rena giggled. "I like your style, too."

Don leaned forward to kiss her and she didn't resist. After a long, passionate kiss, Rena stood up and took Don by the hand. She led him to her bedroom.

SHORTY ROB SAT ON A RICKETY BAR STOOL WITH HIS feet barely touching the floor. The two double shots of Jack Daniels he'd gulped had helped to steady his trembling hands. He considered himself lucky to be alive after his run-in with Don-Don. He needed the whiskey to give him the liquid courage to face the East Side Apostles.

Twenty minutes and two more double shots later, Shorty Rob climbed down from the bar stool. His legs threatened to give way, but he steadied himself by placing his hand on the bar. As soon as the room stopped spinning he made his way to the door.

The brisk Chicago night breeze sobered him up a little—enough to find his car key and climb behind the wheel of his Monte Carlo. The engine choked to life when he turned the key in the ignition. He misjudged the distance between his car and the cars parked in front and the rear of him, bumping them both as he pulled from the parking space. He swerved into traffic and narrowly missed sideswiping a Dodge Intrepid. The man driving the Intrepid honked his horn furiously to get Shorty Rob's attention, displayed an aluminum bat, and sped off.

After the close call with the Dodge, Shorty Rob paid closer attention to his driving. With both hands on the steering wheel he drove like an old woman as he headed for the Nest, an Apostles' hangout. Though he dreaded it, Shorty Rob had to talk to Domino. The thought of pocketing the $10,000 reward wouldn't allow him to chicken out. That and the notion of Rena begging at his feet for him to take her back after they finished with Don made this trip well worth it. He would see how much she wanted to front when he got his hands on that ten gees.

Shorty Rob was so caught up in his grandiose dreams he almost missed his turn. He came back to reality just in time to swerve around the corner where the Nest loomed larger than life.

The Apostles owned and operated the Nest. It was an infamous gathering place for the ghetto's privileged underworld. They also supplied the security and the police were paid to give the place a wide berth.

Shorty Rob found a parking spot and left his car. At the door of the Nest he paid the ten-dollar cover charge and entered the club.

No expense had been spared to furbish the space. The lounge had been decorated to look like a tropical island. Lifelike palm trees with stuffed exotic birds perched on the branches were scattered throughout. The bar itself was a conversation piece—every square inch of its sides and front were covered with the plumage of exotic birds. Sharks and stingrays swam in a thousand-gallon aquarium behind the bar.

Weed fumes hung heavy in the air. The DJ showed a masterful touch as he kept the dance floor packed with willing steppers. As was their custom, the head Apostle sat in a large, plush area behind the dance floor.

Shorty Rob threaded his way through the partygoers to the bar where he ordered a shot of Jack Daniels. When he received his drink he turned his back to the bar and watched the festivities. A pretty girl in a short Coogi dress pressed her chest to the bar next to him. Underneath a pile of weave hair, the girl was more than noticeably attractive, but Shorty Rob tried to remind himself that he was here on business. Under any other circumstances he would have done his best to get her to leave with him.

Turning to her, Shorty Rob asked, "You seen Domino?"

The girl gave him a quick once-over with her red-tinged eyes. She must have decided he wasn't even worth a response because she simply pointed to the area behind the dance floor. He tried to get her name and number for use at a later time, but as he started to lay the groundwork for his mack game, she raised her hand to cut him off. Drink in hand, she retreated and began whispering to her girlfriend. They both looked at Shorty Rob and broke out in laughter.

Shorty Rob was salty—he knew women like her treated poor niggas like that, but he wouldn't be poor for much longer. Mumbling under his breath, Shorty Rob headed in the direction she had shown him. The dance floor was packed. Men and women of all shapes and sizes swayed to a reggae cut. Shorty Rob had to push his way through the crowd to get to the area designated for the Apostles. He received several threatening glares from a few of the dancers he jostled, but he kept moving. Finally he made it to the rear of the club. The atmosphere there was more relaxed. The gang members and their associates sat quietly, smoking blunts, sipping drinks, and talking to women.

Shorty Rob spotted Domino and tried to walk over to the young gangster's booth. Before he knew what was happening, he was facedown on the floor with a pistol behind his ear. Shorty Rob's only response was a whooshing sound from the wind being knocked out of him. One of the gang's security pinned him to the floor with his arm trapped in an excruciating lock. The other held the gun.

"Nigga, who the fuck is you?" the gun-toting security snarled.

"I'm Shorty Rob," he managed to gasp.

"You ain't no Apostle, nigga—we don't know yo ass. What the fuck you want back here?"

"I wanna holla at Domino. Tell him it's about Don-Don."

At the mention of Don's name the man with the pistol stepped over to Domino's booth and whispered in his ear. Domino whispered something back and the security returned and helped Shorty Rob to his feet.

"Domino wanna holla at you," was the only explanation the gun bearer offered as he pushed Shorty Rob through a set of doors to their left. In what had to be a storeroom for the bar, the Apostle instructed him to have a seat on some cases of liquor and he did the same. From his pocket he pulled a blunt and lit it. With a nod of his head he offered Shorty Rob a hit.

Shorty Rob declined his offer. He also noticed the man never put his gun away; though he wasn't so rigid with it, the business end was still pointed at Shorty Rob's stomach. The door opened and two more Apostles entered the room. Like their comrade, they all took seats on the boxes. They passed the blunt around.

There was a knock at the door and one of the men answered it. Shorty Rob hoped it was Domino so he could hurry up and get this shit over with before he lost his nerve. It was only another Apostle bringing the three men some cold drinks. Five more minutes passed before Domino finally entered the storeroom.

Heavily jeweled, sporting a dress shirt, slacks, and alligator shoes, Domino perched on a few cases of liquor.

One of the men waved Shorty Rob silent when he tried to speak.

Domino accepted the blunt. "Alright, little nigga, before you say anything I want you to listen. When my cousin first got killed and I offered a reward for this nigga Don-Don, a million motherfuckas knew where he was at. We followed up on all the tips and we didn't see hide nor hair of this dude. Now, since my time is money, and everybody that sent me on a blank mission wasted my time, that means they also wasted my money. I don't think I got to tell you that pisses me the fuck off. So before you say one word, ask yo'self. Are you telling me the real? And do you want to know what the fuck I'm gone do to you if you not?"

"I seen him," Shorty Rob blurted out. "I seen him in the Wells with a bitch. I talked to the nigga face-to-face. Shit, I was about to kill the nigga myself, but I knew you wouldn'ta liked that. I know it's the same stud because two homicide dicks was showing the nigga picture all over the place. He at this bitch named Rena crib in the Wells. I'll take you to the motherfucka."

Shorty Rob fell silent. He knew he'd captured Domino's attention. A smug look veiled his small, round face. It was said in the streets that pussy was a nigga's quickest downfall and it would prove to be Don-Don's. The nigga shouldn't have tried to steal his girl.

"Awight, Shorty Rob," Domino said, "we gone check this shit out. I hope you ain't lying, little nigga. Breo and Clay, y'all going with me. Clay, go get my truck and bring it round back."

Clay left the storeroom to carry out Domino's order while Breo retrieved two handguns from a mop closet. With the blunt in the corner of his mouth, Breo gave the pistols a quick once-over. He handed Domino a .40 caliber. Outside they heard Clay give a short blow of the truck's horn.

Domino grabbed Shorty Rob by the collar and rudely ushered him out of the door.

The ride to the Wells was a terrifying one for Shorty Rob. He knew the Apostles were used to riding around with heat, but he wasn't. When the nose of Domino's SUV turned into the boundaries of the Wells, Shorty Rob breathed a sigh of relief.

"Where this bitch live?" Clay growled from behind the steering wheel.

"You follow Vincennes to 37th Place, then make a left."

Clay followed the instructions.

"Pull over right here," Shorty Rob ordered meekly.

Noiselessly the 4Runner glided into a parking space a few doors away from Rena's stoop. Domino looked across the backseat at Shorty Rob. "Which one is the bitch crib?"

"Second floor with the yellow curtains."

Domino looked up at Rena's window through the tinted window of his SUV. "Clay, take yo stupid ass around to the back door. Me, Breo, and this nigga going in the front. I'm gone give you three minutes, then I'm going in."

"Hey," Shorty Rob protested. "You ain't say nothing about me going in with y'all. Hell nall. Fuck that!"

A metallic click alerted Shorty Rob that Domino had

cocked the hammer of his pistol. No words were necessary; he got the message.

Clay got out of the truck and headed for the back of the building. Domino and Breo followed Shorty Rob into the building's hallway. They climbed the stairs trying to make as little noise as possible, but Shorty Rob kicked over a discarded forty-ounce bottle. It rolled, tumbled down the stairs, and crashed on the landing. Domino slapped him hard on the back of his head. They continued up the stairs to the second landing and Shorty Rob pointed toward a door. Breo placed his ear to the door and listened for a few moments. He turned and gave the all-clear signal.

Inside the apartment Don was sitting on the couch in his wifebeater and boxers. He had just finished smoking a twenty of crack. He heard the footsteps on the stairs and heard the bottle break, but he didn't become leery until the footsteps paused at the door. There was a small space between the door and the floor and Don could see the movement of the interlopers.

Somebody was trying to sneak up on him.

Quietly, Don scooped up his Python and checked the cylinder. It was fully loaded. He closed the cylinder and sat back to wait.

Outside the apartment Domino gave Breo the go-ahead sign and Breo kicked the door in.

The door gave way easily—so easily that Breo was thrown off balance and stumbled into the living room, dropping his pistol. Without leaving his seat on the couch Don loosed six rounds from his pistol. Four of the six rounds hit Breo in his upper and lower torso, literally ripping him in half at such close range.

Breo tried to scream, but the blood pouring into his lungs drowned him.

Rena was in the bathroom when the apartment door came crashing in. She stepped out and froze as she watched Don butcher the man that blundered through the door.

Domino stepped into the apartment and over Breo. He hesitated only a moment before shooting Rena four times.

Rena's body was flung back into the bathroom, where she staggered backward until she fell into the tub. A hole in her throat made her gasp. Her clutching hands waved back and forth in the air as if she could somehow grasp the air. Finally she grabbed the shower curtain and pulled it down on herself.

Defenseless, Don sat on the couch. His gun was empty. The other bullets were across the room in his pants pocket.

Domino turned his attention to Don. "So, you the notorious Don-Don? You was pretty hard to find. Shit, I actually like yo style. If you wouldn'ta killed my cousin, you the type of nigga that I like to have around me."

At that moment, staring into the darkness of the barrel of Domino's pistol, Don was forced to accept his fate. Even though he didn't know right away who the man's cousin was, he didn't have any doubt that he had killed him.

Calmly, Don pointed to his pipe. "I only want one thing before you lay me down. One last blast."

Don's last request surprised Domino and before he could approve it or deny it, Don picked up his pipe and stuffed the bowl with crack. His lighter flickered and he inhaled the sweet smoke for the last time.

Domino leveled his pistol at Don's head.

Don stared his assassin in the eyes over the rim of his crackpipe.

Two extra-loud gunshots rang out and reverberated.

Don thought his short life was over.

Domino pitched forward onto his face. The back half of his head was a bloody mess.

The boy who had bushwhacked Domino stepped into the room and shot Domino two more times in the head. Bending over Domino's body, the boy examined his handiwork. He removed Domino's necklace and diamond-studded wristwatch.

Don lowered the pipe. "Who you?" Don asked bluntly.

The boy stood up and kicked Domino's body. "Killa Clay. This here nigga used to be my fellow Apostle. I worked for this nigga for four years. He treated me like I wadn't shit. This nigga had a fat truck, got paper, and all that. Me and the rest of his crew walking around without shit.

"This stud was too greedy. Plus he always tried to treat a nigga like a goofy and shit. Trying to make you look like a lame in front of bitches. I been waiting for a chance to get rid of this stud. Yeah, I been playing the send-off man for too long. I know this nigga's operation inside and out. I know where the cash and the product is. I know everything, 'cause I knew I was gone catch this nigga slipping and blow his shit loose. As soon as I heard that you killed his cousin Sajak I knew that my chance was coming. I ain't even gone off you because without you none of this shit would have been possible."

"So what you saying?"

"Nigga, you can beat it. I ain't got no beef with you. One thing, though."

"What's that?"

"I am gone tell the Apostles you killed Domino and Breo, so it may get a teensy bit hectic for you."

"So what if I go to the Apostles and tell them it was you that cooked Domino?"

Clay laughed. "Do you really think they gone believe you over one of their own? Sorry, you got to be the scapegoat in this shit, but I am giving you something in return."

"Oh, yeah? What's that?"

"I'm giving you yo life 'cause you done made me one rich nigga. A, do you know a Shorty Rob?"

"I don't think so."

"Hold on." Clay stepped into the hallway and dragged what appeared to be a dead body into the apartment.

Don recognized the lifeless figure as Rena's ex-boyfriend, the booty-licker. Brain matter oozed out of Shorty Rob's head onto Rena's welcome mat.

"I gave it to him when you was killing Breo," Clay offered. "I hate snitches, you know. Shit, I even get the ten thousand Domino was gone pay this stud for finding you. I guess that's it, Don-Don. I'll see you in hell."

Clay left the apartment.

Don could hear his insane laughter as he left the building.

Taking care not to look at Rena, Don wiped his finger-prints off everything he remembered touching, got dressed, and left the apartment.

IN HER BEDROOM, RHONDA RECLINED ON HER BED AND
tried to study her textbook. She hated economics, but it was
a prerequisite to graduate, so she had to muddle through it
the best she could. Right now she wasn't feeling it. She
threw the book on the floor and rolled over on her side.
Sighing, she shuffled through her stack of CDs. Mary J.
Blige stared up from the case of her CD with a sad look in
her eyes. The lost look on Mary's face mirrored the way
Rhonda felt at this moment. She carefully opened her CD
player and placed the silver disc into it. The soulful sounds
of the ultimate ghetto diva poured into her ears. Tears gathered in her eyes.

Rhonda missed her brother. From her mother, she had

found out that Don was in a lot of trouble. Some of the things they were saying he did were monstrous. On top of that they couldn't find him. He had been gone for days and hadn't so much as called—none of his friends had heard from him, either. She had interrogated them on several occasions to no avail.

Donald didn't think she knew, but she had known for quite a while he was a crackhead. She still loved him, though; she blamed his addiction on Juanita. Ever since Don had brought Juanita home, Rhonda sensed she was no good for her little brother. Trying to talk to Don about her was like talking to a wall—he didn't want to hear it. Their mother was no help at all. Rhonda complained to her whenever she got a chance to see her, but her mother seemed so wrapped up in her job, school, and boyfriend she seemed not to care. In her mother's absence, Rhonda had become the parent, and it was getting to her. The stress of the situation at home began to show in her slipping GPA. Some of her classmates at Chicago State University noticed her academic slump and showed concern. Even though they were close acquaintances, Rhonda chose to remain tight-lipped about her problems. She didn't trust them well enough to let them know what was going on with her little brother. She really didn't know what to do, but she knew that he needed some help. As if Don getting high wasn't bad enough, the other night the police had tried to take the door off the hinges looking for him. They had been polite because her mother was one of them, but they let her know in no uncertain terms that they would be back as often as it took until they found him.

She canceled the events on her social calendar preferring to sit at home, hoping Don would come home or at least telephone. Before the crisis with her brother, all of her energy was channeled into getting her bachelor degree in marketing and advertising. Along the way to reaching her goals she didn't want a baby or a pussy-whipped boyfriend to tie her down, so she was still a virgin. She had came close to having sex on several occasions, but just thinking about her friends who were pregnant or had children had made her back down. For a while the boys who were interested in her continued to call or tried to visit, but she managed to discourage her would-be suitors by keeping a tight grip on her panties.

Across from the Haskill residence, four men sat inside a four-door blue Buick Century. They passed a wicked stick among themselves. The odor of burning formaldehyde and marijuana stunk up the car.

The four men were Juanita's brothers: Tyrone, the second oldest, was the leader; he was a vicious ex-convict and he had dedicated his life to wrongdoing. He had spent so much of his young life behind bars he considered any length of time he spent on the streets as a vacation. His close-set eyes and clean-shaven head added to his psychotic appearance. He loved only a few things in life: crime, his dead sister Juanita, and his youngest brother Johnny.

Johnny was totally subservient to Tyrone. He tried to

emulate Tyrone's every mannerism, his walk, and bald head; he even styled his clothes like his brother. He often wore a bandana around his bald head, looking for all the world like a poor Tupac Shakur. His son had been killed in the fire set by Don. Though he had never relished or even participated in the role of being a father, he still felt anguish at having to bury one of his several children because of Don-Don.

Michael was the oldest brother and Leroy was the second youngest. These two weren't as bright as their brothers, nor did they exhibit the aggressiveness their brothers showed. They were content to bask in the notoriety of their brothers' reputations. If Tyrone told them to do something they would do it, but they never relished the task like Johnny did.

Tyrone and Johnny left the car and cut through the side yard of Don's house to the back door. Leroy and Michael walked up to the front door of the house. Michael rang the doorbell several times—no answer. With a loud whistle, Leroy signaled to his brothers in the rear that it was all clear.

Noiselessly, Tyrone, a master of burglary, broke a glass pane in the door. He stuck his hand through the aperture, being careful not to cut his hand on the jagged remnants of glass, and unlocked the dead bolt. Stealthily, the pair slithered through the open door. On tiptoe they crossed the kitchen and headed to open the front door for their brothers. When everyone was inside they fanned out and searched the first floor.

Their search rendered nothing. Tyrone pointed up the stairs, so they headed for the next level. The first bedroom they tried was empty. The second was Rhonda's. She was sleeping peacefully, clad only in a T-shirt and panties, with her headphones covering her ears.

Tyrone motioned for his brothers to come to the room with the half-naked girl on the bed. A malevolent smile flickered across Tyrone's face. He handed his pistol to Johnny and pulled a knife from his pocket.

"That nigga ain't here," Tyrone whispered. "I bet that's his sister. Let's check this bitch out."

"I don't know," Michael whispered.

"Nigga, is you scared or something?" Johnny whispered scornfully. "Quit acting all soft and shit. Her brother killt our sister and my damn son! Let's get this bitch."

"I know you ain't trying to bitch up on us," Tyrone said to Michael. "Nigga, our motherfucking sister is dead. Now bring you ass on."

Followed by his three brothers, Tyrone stepped into Rhonda's room.

The four brothers surrounded Rhonda's bed. Tyrone snatched the headphones off her head and then woke her with a vicious smack in the mouth.

"Bitch, wake the fuck up, it's party time," Tyrone said.

Rhonda shrieked at the top of her lungs—she was rewarded with a punch in the mouth. She recovered and began to scream again. This time she received a blow to her midsection. Holding her stomach, trying to catch her breath, she looked up at the faces of her attackers. The bald one that hit her in the mouth stepped forward with a knife.

Tyrone used the sharp blade of the knife to slice through the cotton material of her T-shirt and panties.

Rhonda tried to cover up the best she could, but rough hands groped her, tugging and pulling at her flesh. She pressed her thighs together as tightly as possible, but they were too strong for her. They forced her legs open wide and held them open. Rhonda gathered all of her energy.

"HHHHEEEELLLLPPPP!" Rhonda screamed.

The men grabbed her arms, and the one who cut her panties away shoved the shredded underpants in her mouth. The brothers continued with their caresses until Johnny made a startling discovery.

"Damn y'all," Johnny said, his face a mask of wonderment. "This young bitch is a motherfucking virgin!"

"You lying," Tyrone said, doubt all over his face.

Johnny held up his fingers for his brothers to inspect the small amount of blood on them. "For real. I just broke her damn cherry."

"Look out," Tyrone ordered. He positioned himself at the foot of the bed, then kneeled between Rhonda's legs. Using one hand to spread her labia, Tyrone probed her slit with the forefingers of his other hand.

Rhonda screamed into the gag with all her might and wiggled around in protest. She succeeded only in exciting him more.

Tyrone mopped his forehead. "Hold this bitch, y'all. Shit, you wasn't lying. This broad is a motherfucking virgin. She tight than a motherfucka on my fingers." Tyrone paused to sniff his fingers. "Fresh pussy, too. It don't even smell like tuna of the sea. I gots to taste this fucking peach."

Sliding his hands under her thighs, Tyrone cupped her ass and lifted her up to his mouth. He used his tongue to flick her clit back and forth. He started slowly and picked up the tempo. Rhonda struggled and struggled, trying to get him from between her legs.

"Damn, Ty," Leroy commented. "That bitch don't like that shit."

"Shit, that nigga enjoying that pussy samich even if she ain't," Michael quipped.

Tyrone slid one of his hands from under Rhonda and began to slip his fingers in and out of her in unison with his lapping tongue.

Rhonda was so furious at being violated she was huffing and puffing against the gag in her mouth.

Johnny laughed in glee at her displeasure. "Look at this bitch, man! Damn, she mad than a motherfucka at you ass for fucking with that little pearl tongue!"

Tyrone stood up and spit on the floor as he pulled down his pants and boxer shorts. "Goddamnit! Just like a bitch. No matter what you do, they ain't satisfied. You suck a bitch pussy and she still ain't grateful. Well, if she think she ain't like this tongue in that sweet little puss, then she gone hate some of this salami."

Rhonda had closed her eyes, but she opened them wide when Tyrone mounted her and shoved his dick deep inside her. It felt like he was tearing her intestines apart as he recklessly plunged in and out of her. She screamed and screamed into the panties in her mouth, shaking her head from side to side.

Her struggling thrilled Tyrone. He banged away at her like there was no tomorrow for a grand total of three minutes before he shot his load.

"Damn!" Tyrone panted as he stood and wiped his dick on the bedspread. "That's some good shit! It's a little dry, but that's to be expected under the circumstances. You know, first-time jitters. Still, it might be the best shot I ever had. You studs better hurry up and hit it, 'cause I wants me another go-round."

Tyrone pulled up his clothes and went to explore the house for valuables while his brothers took turns raping Rhonda. He was gone for only about fifteen minutes before he returned to Rhonda's room, disgusted. His search of the premises had rendered nothing valuable enough to steal unless they wanted to try and lug a few televisions out to the car. The scene in Rhonda's room reminded Tyrone of a porno movie. Tyrone watched his brothers' sexual antics from the doorway. He decided to wait for a break in the action so he could get a second chance at her.

His brothers had flipped Rhonda on her side. Johnny was obviously enjoying himself as he held one of her arms and plunged his manhood into her womb. Leroy was more sexually adventurous than his brethren, preferring to enter her through the rectum while holding her other arm. Michael was content to masturbate while rubbing her nubile breasts. A few minutes passed and Michael began to climax. With precision he managed to direct the better part of his ejaculate onto Rhonda's face and into her hair.

Rhonda had managed to endure their savage violation of her body until Michael nutted in her face—that was the straw that broke that camel's back. It was the ultimate offense to be raped, but gushing sperm into her face was unbearable. Past worrying about bodily harm, she summoned every iota of her strength and went berserk.

She snatched her arm from Johnny and gave Michael an uppercut in the testicles.

"Funky bitch!" Michael yelped, as he staggered back and clutched his nuts. He fell to his knees and vomited.

Before either brother could react, Rhonda gave Leroy a stiff elbow to the center of his face. The blow made his nose bleed and both of his eyelids began to swell. She raked Johnny across his eyes with her fingernails.

Howling in pain, Johnny grabbed his eyes and fell onto the floor.

Naked, she jumped from the bed and headed for the bedroom door only to find her path blocked by Tyrone. With grim determination she aimed her foot for Tyrone's stomach, but he sidestepped and clamped her leg to his side.

"You know you'se a cute little bitch," Tyrone said. "You got fire, too. I like that shit. It's too bad yo brother killed my sister and my nephew or I would have came back and raped you on a regular basis. Yo pussy was so good and sweet, shit, I hate to do this shit. Damn."

Rhonda saw something glitter in Tyrone's hand. Her brain registered it was a knife. Suddenly she felt tired—there was nothing she could do against four men.

Tyrone grinned. Then he dropped her leg and spun her around quickly. When her back was to his chest he pulled the sharp knife across her jugular vein.

No sound came forth when Rhonda tried to scream. Her throat felt white hot. As her mouth filled with blood she gurgled. She tried to call her mother, brother, or anyone, but her voice box wouldn't obey.

Like a lover breaking the embrace with his woman, Tyrone gently released her. He watched her round ass as she staggered past him into the hallway. He shook his head.

Rhonda made it to the stairway banister before she collapsed. Desperately she tried to recite the Lord's Prayer, but her voice was still on the blink. The pain closed in from all sides, then it began to subside. She finally was able to remember how the Lord's Prayer began, but it was too late.

"OKAY SMITTY, WHAT YOU GOT?" DETECTIVE CARSON grunted as he sipped steaming coffee. He grumbled a string of curses when he scalded his tongue with the scorching liquid. He absentmindedly stubbed a half-smoked Marlboro in an antique china ashtray on the dusty mantelpiece of the brick fireplace. He braced himself to listen to Officer Smith's annoying nasal voice.

The patrolman shifted nervously through his notebook for the relevant details. Smith hated being the first officer on the scene at a homicide—that meant he would have to deal with the homicide dicks.

Officer Smith cleared his throat. "One victim. Female. African American. Her mother is one of ours. She has already identified the deceased as one Rhonda Haskill. Age nineteen. College student. Obviously suffered severe sexual trauma before death. No motive. No known enemies. No boyfriend. Victim was home alone studying. Forced entry. The perp or perps obviously gained entry via the back door. The mother is Sergeant Hazel Haskill, badge number 1372. The father is dead—suicide. The mother found the victim's body. She said there were no vital signs when she found her. We responded to a possible 187 from dispatch."

"Has the coroner been notified?" Detective Winters asked.

"Yes. They're on the way."

"Good work," Winters said before Smith could give her a long answer to a simple question. She put her arm around Officer Smith's soggy shoulders. "What we need you to do is clear everybody out of here. We want the physical evidence to remain intact. I just saw two officers go up the stairs—I need you to get them down here. This is a homicide investigation, and if they contaminate the crime scene they'll receive written reprimands in their files.

"There were some news trucks pulling in when we got here. Keep them curbed. If any one of them crosses the perimeter, arrest them for obstruction. Warn them first. Are the EMTs still upstairs?"

"Yes, but they're just hanging around until the coroner gets here," Smith said.

"Grab us a couple pairs of latex gloves from them. Where is the mother?"

"Sergeant Haskill is sitting on the back porch. We tried

talking to her, but she seems to be in deep shock." Officer Smith smirked and used his index finger to make circles around his ear.

Detective Winters gave him a stony glare and Smith hurried off to find the detectives some examination gloves. He was gone only for a few moments before he returned and handed the detectives the rubber gloves. Smith mumbled something about "crowd control" and left.

"So what do you think, Winters?" Carson asked. "I think it's safe to rule out coincidence. That's just too much luck of the draw for someone to do her after all the shit her brother has gotten himself into."

"Sounds like a reasonable assumption, Carson. I say we take a look at the body, talk to the mother, and see if we can't get a jump on this thing. You know, it's hard when something like this happens to somebody from our side. Next thing you know, you've got half the guys at the precinct ready to wipe out civilians."

"You said it."

The detectives trudged up the stairs. Rhonda's body, covered with a sheet, sprawled a few feet from the top banister. The carpet surrounding her corpse was thick with brown-red clotted blood and the expression frozen on her face seemed like she was gasping for breath.

Carson and Winters knelt beside her body to examine it closely. Carson lifted one of her hands and looked at the fingernails.

"Bingo," Carson said. "Let the lab boys know after the coroner gives us a T.O.D. that we've got some skin under her nails. You see anything?"

"Yeah. Looks like semen in and around her vagina. On her face, too. I think we've got more than one perp unless this guy's tank was full. We'll know for sure when forensics runs some tests. The trail of blood leads into that room."

Winters pointed to Rhonda's bedroom.

The detectives went to check it out. In the room they noted the telltale signs of a struggle—the shredded panties and T-shirt, bed in disarray, and CDs strewn everywhere. Carson almost stepped in Michael's vomit before he noticed it.

"Goddammit, Winters. Look at this. Someone puked. Make sure we have the lab boys bag and tag this shit. If we're lucky and it's the perp's vomit, we might find out where the bastard ate. It's a long shot. . . . There's not much else we can do until they dust the place and do the lab work. Let's have a go at the mother."

Winters followed Carson down the stairs to the back porch. She needed to get her head together before she talked to a fellow officer about the rape and murder of her child. To her, this was always the most difficult part. She hated interviewing the mothers; they always cried and sometimes she would end up crying with them. She found it hard to establish a professional wall between herself and a victim's mother, so she thought it would be best if she let Carson do the talking.

Rhonda's mother sat on the bottom step of the porch. Her white uniform shirt was covered with blood and her copper hair was a mess.

"Sergeant Haskill," Carson said softly but firmly.

There was no way she couldn't have heard him, but she didn't respond.

Carson forged ahead, as was his style. "Sergeant Haskill, I know this is a bad time, but we would like to have a word with you. We want to get these assholes for what they did to your daughter."

Hazel Haskill looked up at the detectives, her eyes slightly out of focus.

"Sergeant Haskill, my name is Detective Carson and this is Detective Winters. I'm really sorry but I have to ask you these questions. We need to know anything that may help us get these guys. Did your daughter have any enemies? Did she ever talk about meeting any new guys?"

Hazel ignored his questions. "My son isn't home and Rhonda is out with her friends. I'm expecting her home at any minute. She knows that she has a curfew and she's really good about keeping it. Rhonda is a good girl. You know she's majoring in business or financing or something. That girl has changed her major so many times I just can't keep up with it."

The female detective crouched down until she was at eye level with Hazel. "Sergeant, Rhonda is dead. We're trying to find out who did this. Do you understand?"

"When you see Don-Don, you tell him I'm going to whup his behind," Hazel said dreamily. "The nerve of that boy. It's bad enough that he started getting high, now he done went and got his sister killed. Now how is she gone pass her midterms? I'm going to beat that boy's butt real good. That's what he need. I can't wait until his father gets home. I'm going to tell him he better do something with that boy before I send him to Job Corps or somewhere."

Carson gently pulled Winters to her feet. He signaled it was time to leave; Sergeant Haskill could offer them no assistance in her condition. When they left the porch she was mumbling something about her husband.

The forensics team had arrived with their bags, powders, and cameras. Winters gave them instructions while Carson looked on. When she was through the detectives headed for their car.

In the car Winters sighed. "I hate to see this type of shit. No matter how many times it happens, I'll never get used to it. These guys have got to be inhuman to do what they did. One thing we do know is that when Don gets word of this—and he will"—she nodded at the reporters berating the patrolmen for not letting them past the yellow tape—"he's going to come out of hiding. He'll show his face and we'll be waiting."

DON WAS BORED AS HELL IN HIS CASKET-SIZED ROOM AT the Zanzibar Motel.

Television was his only link to the outside world. The programming wasn't the greatest, but it gave him something to do besides smoking crack. News programs were his favorite. He loved the lopsided reporting of the networks—all drug raids, murders, and atrocities against children. It was no wonder other races perceived Blacks as animals, thanks to the daily reports.

Smoking crack was even getting boring—not that he was considering abstinence. It would have been nice to have someone to talk to. He actually found himself missing Juanita. For the thousandth time since her death, Juanita crossed his mind. In the short time he had known her, she had changed his whole life. He was nothing like the person he used to be, thanks to her. Most of this shit was her fault. If it wasn't for her, he wouldn't be on the run now. Before she died she had transformed him into a complete crack monster. Rena crossed his mind, too. She seemed like she would have really been easy to get along with, but in a heartbeat she was gone, too. Rena hadn't been anything like Juanita. She wasn't motivated by crack rocks so she was still able to express genuine emotion. Just the fact that she didn't care if he smoked but wouldn't touch the stuff herself made him respect her. If she had lived, it wasn't like he was going to try and turn her out either. The last thing he needed was another Juanita.

Don wished that he could get revenge for Rena's death. She was a sweet soul who was murdered for no reason other than that she had met him. Now she had been shot down in the prime of her life by somebody seeking revenge for a murder that Don didn't even commit. There was no one to retaliate against—the Apostle Clay had seen his opportunity and seized it, murdering Domino and leaving Don without an outlet for his sense of rage and loss. Don knew he couldn't strike at Clay. He owed the fact that he was still breathing to Clay, but that was a double-edged sword, because he knew that the Apostles were probably already hunting him in the streets.

It was too hot for him in Chi-town. His best bet would be to get out of the frying pan.

Minnesota seemed to be calling him. Everybody seemed

to be migrating to St. Paul and Minneapolis anyway. Since he really couldn't picture himself living in some one-horse, backwater town in Mississippi, somewhere north seemed like the best option. It would be easy for him to lose himself among the millions of people there. Copping crack definitely wouldn't be a problem—lots of dealers from the city had moved there because it was a fresh market for crack.

He wasn't leaving much behind, only his sister and mother. All of his friends were gone, Juanita was dead, and now Rena.

Don picked up his pipe. It was time to stop thinking. He didn't need to get emotional in such a tight space. Trying to shut down his brain, Don packed the bowl of his whistle and sucked it clean.

Pipe in hand, he turned on the television. He flicked through the channels until he came to the evening news. After five minutes he was about to change the channel when the newscast switched from the studio to a female reporter broadcasting live on location; the location was his mother's house. His address flashed across the screen as the reporter droned on. Don turned up the volume as the screen flashed to a high-school graduation picture of his sister. Stunned, Don listened to the reporter.

A gust of wind blew the Latin reporter's long hair in her face. "We're here live at 6417 South Langley, the scene of a grisly murder. Nineteen-year-old Rhonda Haskill has been positively identified as the victim. From what we have been able to glean from a source in Area 1, the young woman was raped and murdered by an unknown number of suspects.

"Evidently, Rhonda struggled with her assailants and was murdered during the struggle. As of yet the coroner hasn't established the time of death. Her body was found by Hazel Haskill, a forty-two-year-old desk sergeant at Area 2 headquarters. Rhonda was . . ."

In a blind rage Don kicked the television off the stand. His vision blurred for a second. When his eyes focused again Don caught sight of his pipe. His hands trembled as he dropped ready rocks onto the screen of the pipe and took a blast. Beads of sweat appeared on his forehead as he emptied the bowl.

Don blew out white smoke and laughed. "That reporter ho is lying. That wadn't my motherfucking house. That's some bullshit."

Laughing, he fell back on the bed. Incessant banging on the room door dried up his insane laughter.

"Open this gotdamn door!"

Don recognized the disembodied voice of the motel manager.

"What's wrong?" Don asked without opening the door.

"Nigga, I know yo ass is trying to steal the TV! I done already called the police! I said open this damn door!"

Don realized too late that in any cheap motel if you unplugged the television an alarm sounded in the manager's office. He collected his pistol, pipe, and crack and dipped into the bathroom. The window opened easily and Don dropped out of it onto some rubbish in the alley.

Through a crack in the boards of the fence surrounding the motel he saw a blue and white patrol car pull up in front of the manager's office. He could hear the irate manager beckoning to them from in front of his room door. The two officers catapulted from the car and headed for the stairwell.

Don turned and ran up the alley until he reached 67th Street. On 67th he walked west to Cottage Grove. There he sat on a bench at the bus stop. He really didn't need to rest; he needed a blast. With total disregard for the few people waiting for the bus, Don smoked a bowl of crack.

His close brush with the law had made reality smack him in the face. His sister was dead. The only thing he could do was try and find out who did the deed. He would have to go home and talk to his mother. It was a long shot, but she might know something. Maybe the police had told her something. It might have been insignificant to them, but it could be just enough of a clue for him to find out who did this shit to his sister.

The bus pulled up and everyone got on, except for Don. He took another hit of crack. He decided that he needed a ride, not a bus ride, but in somebody's car. He walked to the corner and waited for someone to pull up to the light. After several light changes, still no luck. The traffic light turned red again and his pigeon pulled up to the light.

A female driver in a gold Toyota Cressida sat at the light, bobbing her head to music.

Careful not to attract her attention, Don eased his pistol out and stepped off the curb. He dashed to the driver's side door and yanked it open.

"Bitch, get out my car!" Don snarled, putting his gun to her head.

The scared woman made a move to try and peel off.

With his free hand Don cocked the hammer of his pistol and then grabbed her dreadlocks.

"Ho, if you get out now you'll live to drive again," Don threatened.

This time she saw the logic in Don's approach and threw the gearshift in park. She got out in the middle of Cottage Grove.

Don jumped in the car, slammed the door, and made a U-turn in the intersection. His last glimpse of the woman was of her sitting on the bus-stop bench with her head in her hands. He left the radio volume loud as he peeled up Cottage Grove. At 71st Street he turned the radio down in front of the police station and turned west, heading for King Drive. On King Drive he swung a right and sped down to 63rd Street.

He was going home, but first he needed to check out a few things. On 63rd Street he parked the Cressida and hopped out. After making sure the butt of his pistol was in plain view, he strolled into his old hangout.

The game room was packed. As Don walked to the rear of the establishment, anyone near the front door thinned out. In the rear of the game room there were a few new faces and some regulars. Carlos was there, and his appearance since the last time Don had seen him had totally changed. He had on new shoes, new clothes, and a half-carat diamond shone in his ear. Carlos was perched on some milk crates talking on a cellular phone.

When Carlos looked up and saw Don standing over him, he stuttered for a few seconds more into his cell phone and then ended the call.

"What's up, 'Los?" Don asked evenly. He had been extra careful to make sure there was no animosity in his voice when he spoke.

Carlos didn't sense any malice in Don's voice so he decided to play along and see where the conversation took them. He knew Don had to have heard about his sister. That was the only reason he could see for his old friend to be on the set as hot as his name was.

"Nothing to it, but to do it," Carlos replied.

"I ain't on no bullshit, Carlos. I just want to holler at you about some shit real quick."

Carlos stood up. As he followed Don toward the door he slipped his hand into his jacket pocket to grip his .380 Super. Clicking the safety off, Carlos decided it was better to be safe than sorry. He closely watched every movement Don made as he followed him outside.

Don sat on the hood of his freshly jacked car and lit a cigarette. "Like I said, 'Los, I ain't on no bullshit. I just want to know what the word on the bricks is about my sister. I got to get the . . ." Don stopped talking because his voice was shaking. He looked away so Carlos wouldn't see the tears in his eyes.

Carlos looked away too. "We been looking for the motherfuckas, too. That was some bogus shit. Rhonda was like a big sister to us, too. We been knowing her since we was shorties coming to get you for school. She ain't never hurt nobody. That nigga Dre snapped when he heard the news. We tore the Tray up and 61st, but don't nobody know shit. Dre wanna see you, man. Yo moms, too. We looking for the studs, too. You gone be alright?"

"I'm straight," Don said as he walked around to the driver's side of the Cressida. "Imma bump heads with y'all later. I got to go check on some shit."

Don got in the car and peeled out.

In his wake Carlos hopped in his Seville and whipped out his cellular. "Dre, this is 'Los. Don was just up here at the game room. Yeah, he look crazy than a motherfucka. Smoked out and shit. Hell, yeah. He ain't on no bullshit, though. Yeah, he heard about Rhonda. He ready to hurt something. He ain't say where he was going, but he driving a little gold Toyota. Alright, Imma call you back later."

21

DETECTIVES WINTERS AND CARSON SAT IN THEIR UN-marked police vehicle sipping coffee from a Thermos. They were parked half a block away from the Haskill residence and trying to be as inconspicuous as possible. So far the night had proved uneventful. Bad vibes after the grisly murder of Rhonda Haskill had the block's residents barricading themselves in their homes before the streetlights flickered on.

Around ten p.m., a dark blue Buick Century with tinted windows drove down the block. It pulled into a parking space across the street from the Haskill house. Ten minutes passed and the passengers still remained in the car.

Winters sat forward and squinted at the Buick. "Winters, that Century. Nobody got out. I can't make out how many passengers through that fucking tint."

Using field binoculars, Carson took a look at the mid-sized sedan. He gave the Buick, and the street, a good look. He placed the binoculars back on the seat and reached for his cup of coffee.

"Looks normal, Winters. I can't see any movement. Probably just some horny kids out for a quickie in mom's car."

Winters kept her eyes on the Buick as she reached for the radio. "I don't know, Carson. It may be nothing, but I think I'll have a blue and white roll through. If that doesn't clear them up, then we need to do an 'approach and interview.' "

Carson put his hand over Winters' hand on the radio. He let it remain there for a few seconds longer than he should have.

"Don't do that, Winters. I'm telling you, it's nothing. Just a couple of kids. It would be just our luck that Donald shows and sees a squad car. That'll scare him off for certain. Don-Don is coming. I know he's heard about his sister's death by now. We can't blow a stakeout in a major homicide case because a couple of kids were smoking dope or playing touchy-feely. We're already getting dragged over a cheese grater because we haven't produced this kid. C'mon now, Winters, stay focused."

Winters released the radio and sat back. *Maybe he's right,* she thought. *I'm probably just antsy from sitting so long.*

In the blue Buick Century, Juanita's brothers waited to ambush Don-Don. Tyrone sat at the steering wheel and

Michael filled the passenger seat; Johnny and Leroy occupied the backseat. They had returned every night since they'd murdered Rhonda. In between snorts of raw cocaine and puffs of wicked stick, they watched the house and the street.

"Stop hogging all the motherfucking coke, Lee!" Johnny said. "Ty, tell that nigga to stop trying to toot the whole motherfucking shit!"

Leroy looked up with white powder on the tip of his broad, brown nose. "Nigga, quit crying to Ty. Ty ain't my damn daddy. You always trying to coordinate the high and shit. Shit, I put up just as much as you on this shit. Ty, tell this nigga to shut the fuck up."

With the embalming-fluid-dipped joint hanging out of the corner of his mouth, Tyrone said, "Both of you niggas need to shut the fuck up. Why don't you niggas stop acting like some bitches over that coke shit. That's why I don't even like snorting that white girl. Motherfuckas be ready to kill each other over some funky-ass powder. Shit taste like aspirin anyway. Lee, pass the motherfucking shit, before I have to whup one of y'all ass."

Leroy took one more quick toot and then handed the sandwich bag to his brother. Like his brother, Michael preferred to smoke wicked sticks instead of snorting cocaine. He liked the crazy courage the formaldehyde gave him.

Half an hour after the brothers had parked their car, a gold Cressida zoomed up and whipped into the parking space in front of the Haskill house. Without turning the car off the driver peered around for a few seconds and got out of the car.

"It's him, that got to be him," Johnny hissed excitedly. "I told y'all the nigga would come!"

Leroy reached down to the shoe box at his feet and pulled out four pistols. He gave one to each of his brothers, keeping one for himself. Leroy and Johnny were prepared to exit the vehicle blasting, but Tyrone stopped them.

Tyrone craned his neck to peer through the passenger window. "Hold fast, y'all. What the fuck is this nigga doing? Can you see, Johnny?"

Johnny didn't have to answer.

After parking the Cressida, Don looked up and down the block. The set seemed clear so he got out of the car, sat on the hood, and whipped out his pipe. He dropped a few small rocks into the pipe and used his lighter to get rid of them.

Down the street the detectives watched in disbelief as Don smoked the crack. All the time they had been after him they thought he was a heavyweight drug dealer, not a crackhead.

"Look at this jerk, Winters. This son-of-a-bitch has got balls. He's smoking dope right in front of his mother's house." Carson's face was red as he handed his partner the field glasses. "Are you ready to get this asshole?"

Don was tapping his quickly cooling pipe on his leg to remove any loose residue. The gold Cressida gleamed in the night as Don left the hood and headed for the steps of his house.

When Don's back was to the street the four doors of the Buick Century opened and Juanita's brothers oozed out of the car.

Detective Carson had removed his .38 from the holster and was prepared to exit the vehicle when Winters placed her hand on his arm.

"Hold on, Carson," Winters said, the binoculars to her eyes. "There's some extra players on the field and they don't look like they play fair. Take a look."

Carson accepted the binoculars. "Who the hell are these punks? Looks like they're after our guy, too. Goddammit, these street punks could take over a small country with all that hardware! Winters, call for backup. No sirens, no lights. Undercovers already on the scene. Hold on, they're saying something to Donald." Carson stealthily crept from the car.

"Don-Don, what's up, baby boy!" Tyrone shouted.

Don turned to see who was hailing him. Instinctively his hand went to his pistol butt in his waistband. He could just make out four shadows across the street.

"Who dat?" Don asked, shading his eyes from the porch light. "Come out so I can see you."

One of the figures stepped off of the opposite curb and walked to the middle of the street. Don looked the man up and down; he didn't recognize him.

"I don't know you, homie. You got the wrong man." Don turned to continue about his business when he sensed rather than saw the man in the street up a pistol.

"But you know my little sister, Juanita!" Tyrone yelled, a split second before he began blasting.

Don had begun to move as soon as he felt the man pull the pistol. He dived behind the concrete railing of the front porch with his .357 barking. As he lay behind the railing he could hear the sound of different guns firing as the other men joined the gun battle. Slugs from his attackers dug into the wall behind him and shattered windowpanes, showering Don with brick chips and shards of glass.

When they finally gave him a breather, Don shouted, "A, homie, I didn't even touch yo sister! She got hit by a damn truck trying to run across the street!"

Don couldn't tell if he got his point across because he heard a voice yell, "Freeze!" There weren't any bullets flying so he peeked from behind his hiding spot. There was a white man in the middle of the street, obviously a detective, pointing a gun at the four men who had just tried to kill him.

"Drop the fucking guns and get facedown!" Detective Carson ordered.

The four men were on the verge of complying when a car careened around the corner, practically on two wheels, distracting the detective. The Park Avenue rocketed up the block and screeched to a stop behind the stolen Cressida.

Tyrone saw the detective was off balance. Instead of laying his gun on the ground, Tyrone shot from the hip. The first shot missed completely, but the second smashed into Carson's jaw. A volley from Johnny's gun hit Carson in his chest, breaking two of his ribs.

Dre leaped from the Park Avenue with a pistol in each hand and began spitting leaden balls of death at Juanita's brothers. His entry came as such a surprise, he had shot Michael and grazed Johnny before they recovered and ducked for cover, firing all the while.

Dre's interference gave Don the diversion he needed to make his getaway. Not that he wanted to run from the gun-fight—he just didn't want to be around when the police made the scene and found one of their comrades shot. Don knew from the way the detective fell he had to be dead or hurt real bad. He knew they would find some way to blame it on him just like everything else. With self-preservation foremost in his mind, Don crawled off the porch, across the lawn, and through the passenger door of the quietly purring Cressida. As he was sliding over into the driver's seat he peeked to see what was going on.

Winters knelt on one knee, swept her hair out of her eyes, and shot Dre in the back. Dre pitched forward onto his face in the middle of the street. Shots rang out from behind the cars on the opposite side of the street and Winters had to scamper for cover. She returned the bushfire, but Juanita's brothers kept her pinned down.

Then the cavalry began to arrive. The first police vehicle swerved onto the block as Don was putting the Cressida into gear. Don saw the police car in his rearview mirror and mashed on the gas.

The police car gave chase to the gold car.

Don whipped around the corner and sped up the next block going the wrong way. In the rearview mirror he saw that two more police cars had joined the chase. Now their lights were flashing and their sirens were blaring. As he sped up one street and down another, the Toyota he was driving held its own, but he knew it couldn't outrun their Motorola walkie-talkies. Surrendering was the furthest thing from his mind, but he knew a long car chase wouldn't be beneficial either—he was already on the lookout for a place to bail.

Trying to get enough distance between him and the police cars so he could jump out, Don deftly maneuvered the sedan like a stunt driver down sidewalks, through vacant lots, on side streets, mostly in the wrong direction. It took all of his skill to avoid wiping out on several occasions. Throwing caution to the wind he flew east on 63rd Street and busted a tight donut in the busy intersection. He swerved to avoid hitting a lady crossing the street with her child, and shot off in the opposite direction.

Don's sudden 360-degree turn started a chain-reaction accident. The blue and white police car directly behind him tried to make the U-turn on the dime, but the heavier Chevy skidded and slid into the oncoming traffic. The second police car crashed into an iron El train support beam. The third car rear-ended the second car and pushed it into a storefront on the corner. Not even taking time to watch the police cars crash and burn, Don sped west on 63rd Street, making a sharp right. He pulled into the alley and bailed from the car. Quick as a jackrabbit he scampered through a gangway and across the street. Police sirens wailed as he made his way into another gangway. He fled through a vacant lot.

This is my turf, he thought. *There's no way I'm gonna let some slow, donut-munching motherfucka catch me in my own jungle.*

He ran across King Drive and into another vacant lot. He ran through a gangway. At the end of the gangway a large, vacant building loomed in the darkness like an ancient temple. Don slipped through the fence surrounding the building, ignoring a *Keep Out Demolition in Progress* sign. He went past a large, waste-hauling container to the building's boarded entryway. With a mighty heave, he ripped the board off the yawning entrance.

Dank, musty air slapped him in the face. Don stepped out of the night and into the hallway. He pulled the board back across the mouth of the doorway. Using his cigarette lighter to illuminate the way, Don ran up the creaking, protesting staircase to the third floor. Randomly he picked an apartment and kicked the door open. He went from room to room of the large apartment until he found one with the least amount of garbage strewn on the floor.

The adrenaline rush from his close brush with death and the law had subsided. Exhausted from his adventures, Don slumped on the wall and slid to a sitting position on the floor. Now that he was alone he took a hit of crack and tried to sort out the night's events.

Things were happening fast. Since the news of his sister's death, he had been evicted from his motel room, carjacked someone, been shot at by Juanita's brothers, watched his best friend be gunned down, and been the prey in a high-speed car chase. Now he was holed up in an abandoned building. *That was what you called sliding down a razor blade into an alcohol river,* he thought.

Things were so fucked up that he seriously considered eating a bullet. It sounded like an easy way out, but Don knew deep down inside that was a punk's way out. A real nigga could go through twice the shit he was going through and never once consider snuffing his own candle. Suicide wasn't the answer. If he was right, he had just found his sister's killers, or they had found him. For now they would have to wait. He would just have to chill for a few days and then try to make it out of town and come back at a later date to try and avenge his sister's death.

DON KNEW IT WAS TIME TO MOVE ON AFTER HIS THIRD night of hiding. He was so hungry it felt as if his stomach was touching his spine. Disheveled, musty, and thirsty, he felt like death warmed over.

At first he planned to stop at his house only long enough to see his mother one last time and let her know he was leaving town. Now he had altered that plan to include a hot shower, change of clothes, and a meal. He didn't really need any money, but maybe he could hit his mother up for a few bucks.

Don walked to the window and looked out for the umpteenth time. The streets were quiet. As he gathered his meager belongings, something reminded him that he would have to miss his sister's funeral. Rhonda . . . He was absolutely sure that anyone and everyone looking for him would be there. One last time he needed to see her. Rhonda . . .

Over the three nights of solitude he had managed to piece together the puzzle his life had become. Juanita's brothers had to be the ones who raped and killed Rhonda; a senseless murder in retaliation for their sister's death. It made him angry every time he thought about it. Juanita. Thieving, crackhead bitch. Her life was nothing to exchange for Rhonda's. If he thought for a moment that anyone would have gone after his sister, he would have killed them first. He knew he couldn't get Juanita's brothers now. Any of them who had survived the shoot-out were more than likely in police custody or on the run.

With tears in his eyes, Don took a blast before leaving the security of his stronghold. As the crack burned in the pipe bowl, he watched the smoke swirl through the glass bowl to his lips. Smoking crack made him think. A lifetime ago he would have been smoking blunts, hooping, and sharing a cold beer with his buddies. How he transformed from an easygoing youth into a killer crackhead was beyond him.

Don was tempted to smash his pipe against the tenement wall. He wanted to dump the rest of his crack out the window, but the hype inside him wouldn't allow it. The reality of what he had become was too much to deal with. The tears were coming hard and fast now. Rhonda and Dre . . . Juanita and Rena . . .

Almost blinded by the salty fluid, Don crashed out of the apartment and half-ran, half-jumped down the three flights of stairs. He kicked the board and ran out of the building. Across the street, he hopped a gate and ran through the yard.

A snarling Rottweiler loomed from the darkness, barking and growling. Reflex brought Don's pistol to his hand. He pumped a nickel-sized slug into the dog's broad chest as it leapt at him. Mercilessly, Don shot the retreating canine in its haunches and then climbed out of the yard. Driven by grim determination, Don ran and ran until he collapsed on the back stairs of his own house. As his ragged breathing slowed, he whipped out his pipe, packed the bowl, and revitalized his ebbing strength with a mega-blast.

When his head stopped swimming enough for him to stand without collapsing, Don staggered up the stairs and rang the doorbell. There was no answer to his incessant ringing so he stuck his hand through the broken window-pane and turned the dead bolt lock. The door opened.

His mother was sitting at the kitchen table with her eyes closed. Obviously the half-empty liter of Seagram's in front of her had been keeping her company. Don had never known his mother to take a drink, but it looked like she'd had half a liter of gin. Her hair was unkempt and a foul odor, even worse than his own smell, wafted up from her. Her white shirt was covered with dried blood and filth. She

was so intoxicated he didn't even think she was aware of his
presence until she spoke.

"Come on in, Donald," Hazel Haskill slurred. "I been
waiting on you."

Don took a step closer. He was scared of his mother for
the first time in his life. He didn't like the sound of her voice.
Nevertheless, Don made his way around the table and
kissed her on her unwashed cheek. Up close, the smell of alcohol and blood threatened to overpower him. Don took a
seat across from her and tried to feel her out.

"Hey, Momma. How you doing? Taking a little time off
from work, huh? It's about time. You need the rest."

Hazel Haskill never answered her son's patronizing questions. Soon a stony silence blanketed the room.

Don went over to the fridge. Before he opened it he read
a piece of paper in some stranger's handwriting that gave the
date and time for his sister's funeral. The funeral was tomorrow, but the body could be viewed tonight. Making a mental note of that, Don opened the refrigerator. There were
some cold cuts so he made himself a huge sandwich. A cold
Pepsi and plain potato chips made his sandwich into a meal.
His mother never said a word as he sat at the table to devour
his meal.

While eating, he looked up once or twice because he
could feel his mother's eyes boring holes in his skull. As he
polished off the food, she never opened her mouth except to
pour more gin down her throat. When he was through eat-

ing, Don sat back in his chair and fired up a cigarette. His mother didn't even say anything about him riding back in her chair. Don finished his cigarette and dropped the butt into the Pepsi can. He was tired of sitting there feeling stupid so he got up.

"Momma, I'm finta go take me a shower. Do you need me to do anything for you?"

Before she answered, his mother dumped a shot of gin in her mouth. "No, Arthur. Rhonda is going to wash the dishes and Donald will empty the garbage when he comes in. I know you had a long day at work, so you go ahead and take your shower. I'll come in a little later and give you a back rub."

Don was stupefied. His mother had referred to him as Arthur. Arthur was his father's name. His mother had also spoken about Rhonda as if she was still alive.

"Momma, Rhonda and Arthur, I mean Daddy, are dead. They're both gone."

His mother looked up at him. For a brief moment the light of sanity tried to break through the murkiness of her mind. "Oh, I keep forgetting. I'm sorry, Donald. Go ahead and get cleaned up."

Don pushed his chair under the table and kissed his mother on the cheek again. In the bathroom he smoked a rock while he waited for the shower to get hot. He sat naked on the side of the tub and blew the smoke toward the ceiling. The water was warm enough now so he stepped under it. The hot beads of water felt good on his exhausted body.

He worked up a good lather with the deodorant soap. The bathroom door opened. There was soap on Don's face so he couldn't open his eyes.

"Momma, I'm in here!" Don yelled.

"I know, Arthur. I just came in here to keep you company," his mother said in a sultry voice. She pulled back the shower curtain and stepped into the tub.

Don stuck his head under the shower nozzle to get the soap off his face. He wiped his eyes with a washcloth. His mother, completely naked, stood behind him. He cringed, trying to cover his manhood with the towel.

"Arthur, I know how much you like to make love in the shower," his mother cooed.

Don couldn't believe it; his mother really thought he was his father. She came close to try and fit under the shower-head with him. Her naked breasts touched him as she reached for his manhood and Don recoiled. He tried to get out of the tub, but his mother grabbed his arm.

"Where you going, Arthur?"

Yanking his arm out of her grasp made him slip and he had to grab the shower curtain to avoid falling on his face. He righted himself and sprang out of the tub. He grabbed his things and fled from the bathroom. He bolted up the stairs to his bedroom and locked the door. Dripping wet, he flung himself on the bed. Tears of anger and frustration assaulted his eyes. His mother came to his bedroom door.

"Donald, Donald, I'm sorry!" she screamed as she pounded on the door. "Arthur, I'm sorry! I didn't mean to bother you! I just wanted you to make love to me before the kids came home! Let me in, baby, and I'll do whatever you like!"

His mother was hysterical and her ranting and raving only made him more emotional. Don stood up and walked over to the door. He leaned his forehead against the cool wood. "Go away, Momma," he sobbed. "Momma, I'm not Arthur, I'm Donald. Rhonda is dead, Momma. Just go away."

The pounding at his door stopped. Don knew his mother hadn't left because he could hear her weeping on the steps. He sat on the bed and tried to block out the memory of what happened in the shower, but the memory of it was too fresh. Don dug through his wet, dirty clothes and whipped out his pipe and crack. With trembling fingers he packed the pipe bowl with a dub-sized rock. Waving his cigarette lighter like a magic wand over the bowl, he let the crack melt a little and then took a godfather hit. He packed the bowl again and held the torch to it. Inside him, the smoke felt like it was curling around his brain, keeping him warm and cooling him off at the same time.

Don sat the hot pipe on his nightstand as jabs of pain shot through his left arm and shoulder. He stumbled to his closet and pulled out some pants and a shirt. In his dresser he found some socks and underwear and stepped into them. He dried his tears on his shirt, stuffed his pipe and crack into his pocket, and put his pistol in his waistband. He opened his door, stepped over his weeping, naked mother, and jumped down the stairs. In the kitchen he grabbed his mother's keys off the counter and snatched the funeral information from the refrigerator door. Not looking back, he slammed the back door.

23

DETECTIVE WINTERS SAT IN THE BACK OF THE SMALL chapel. Her face was partially hidden by a Bible, but she was totally aware of her surroundings. She had been there since the funeral director opened the door for the viewing. There had been a few relatives—none of them were of any interest to her. It was a long shot, but a lot of crimes were solved on a long shot. Winters knew the chance of Don-Don showing up here was slim or none. If he did show she would keep calm and wait for backup.

This was one of the wildest cases she'd had the displeasure of working. Her partner was in serious but stable condition. Three more guys were dead and she didn't have a clue to what Donald Haskill's role was in all of this. She would find out, though. If he came to view the body or showed up at the funeral tomorrow, Winters vowed that this would come to an end.

Two young men walked into the chapel, causing Winters to slouch down in her seat. They signed the visitors' book and approached the casket. Both men wore jackets with fraternity insignias on them. Both men stood quietly in front of the casket for a few moments. One of them bravely brushed his lips against Rhonda's cold forehead. The man stood and his eyes swept about the room. He noticed the gigantic bouquet of flowers from the Chicago Police Department and pointed them out to his friend. The two men whispered between themselves for a moment, turned, and left.

A small, white woman with silver-gray hair strode into the chapel. On her hair was perched a pair of reading glasses. The woman never walked up to the coffin. She took a seat in the front row and sat quietly for about ten minutes. Her lips moved silently as if in prayer, she stood and crossed herself, and left without signing the visitor book.

Winters looked at her watch. It was forty minutes to closing. She had resigned herself to hoping Don would show at the funeral when he suddenly walked through the door. Thrills of alarm ran through Winters as he strode to the casket. Slouching even farther in her seat, Winters slid her pistol out of the holster. She shielded it on her lap with the Bible as two young girls walked into the chapel. The girls stopped to sign the visitors' book. Seeing Don at the coffin, they took a seat in the rear of the chapel. Winters returned her attention to Don at the casket. Great sobs shook the boy's frail body. Winters left her seat and eased up a few rows closer to the casket.

"Rhonda, don't leave me," Don wailed as he held his sister's lifeless hand. "I'm so sorry, I'm sorry, Rhonda. Rhonda, please don't leave me and Momma."

Don knelt on the small stool in front of the casket and kissed his sister's cold hand.

It would have been a touching scene to Detective Winters, but she knew the boy kneeling at his sister's casket was a killer. Still concealing her pistol behind the Bible, Winters left the chapel and, for lack of a better place, she closeted herself in the two-stall women's bathroom. She didn't like letting Don out of her sight, but she needed to call for backup.

"This is Homicide Detective Winters," she whispered into her radio. "I have spotted a murder suspect and I need backup. I'm in the chapel of A. R. Leak Funeral Home on 78th and Cottage Grove. Be advised suspect is armed and dangerous, approach with extreme caution. Detective will be maintaining radio silence. Copy?"

"That's a copy," was the dispatcher's static response.

Winters tucked her radio in her blazer and readjusted the Bible and pistol. In the chapel she was relieved to see Don was still on his knees by the casket. A glance let her know the two girls were still waiting to view the body. Choosing an aisle seat this time, Winters sat and watched Don grieve.

Finally, Don stood and wiped his face. Winters knew she would have to make her move, with or without backup. As she was ready to spring into action she heard the girls gasp loudly. Winters looked back over her shoulder and saw two men advancing toward the casket. One of the men was limping and the other had a large bandage on his neck. The one with the limp carried a sawed-off shotgun; the other carried a small handgun. They walked straight down the aisle toward Don, not paying any attention to the girls or Winters.

Fear turned Winters' stomach muscles into knots. These were two of the men who were outside of Don's house when her partner was shot. Two were killed, but these two had gotten away when the backup squad chased Donald and crashed their cars.

"We caught yo bitch ass," Johnny said, aiming the shotgun at Don's back.

Don wheeled around with a look of shock on his face. He put his hands up. "Hold up, man. I don't even know you niggas."

Johnny sneered. "Stud, you ain't got to know us. Bitch, you killed our motherfucking sister."

"I ain't kill yo sister. She ran in front of a truck. I was just trying to get my cola back from her ass. She didn't even look and tried to run across Cottage. I wasn't even gone put my hands on her. She stole my shit, though."

"We ain't trying to hear that shit," Leroy said. "Our brothers is dead, too, cause of yo ass, nigga. Fuck this nigga, Johnny."

Don could see the muscles in Johnny's face tighten as he prepared to squeeze the trigger. A second too late Don dove over the casket. The loud boom of the shotgun in the chapel was deafening. Shotgun pellets peppered Don's side and back and embedded themselves in the side of Rhonda's casket.

Winters sprang into action. She dropped the Bible and stood.

"Freeze! Drop your weapons!" Winters yelled.

Leroy tried to spin around, but the wound in his neck made his move awkward and cumbersome. By the time he brought the .25 semiautomatic around, Winters squeezed off two shots from her pistol, smacking into his chest a millisecond after one another. Leroy flipped face-first onto a pew. Johnny turned and loosed the other barrel of the shotgun in Winters' face. Most of the pellets lodged in her bulletproof vest, shredding her blouse as they passed through it. One pellet grazed her eyebrow and another entrenched itself in her cheek.

Winters flew backward in the aisle. Her gun fell out of her hand as she landed on her back. She groaned and grabbed her chest. Johnny emptied the two spent shells from the shotgun and retrieved two more from his pocket as he advanced on Winters.

Don crawled from behind his sister's casket and began to crawl under the pews. His gun was in his hand and his side and back ached, so it was a difficult task. He made it to the row where the two girls had been sitting. They were crouched on the floor hugging one another. Don put his finger to his lips and crawled past them. He could see Johnny's feet as Johnny stood over Winters, loading the shotgun.

"Pig bitch, you keep getting in our business," Johnny said. "You just killed another one of my brothers, bitch. I'm glad you was here because you saved us the trouble of having to come after yo ass. Oh, you can bet we was coming. This way is better, though. I get to kill two birds with one stone."

Johnny snapped the shotgun closed and aimed it at Winters' head. Don wanted to keep crawling, but as he drew parallel to Winters on the floor he could see the look of fear on her face. Don knew what he had to do. Leaning on one arm he aimed the pistol at Johnny's head and pulled the trigger.

Reflex made Johnny fire the shotgun as he fell over on his side. Portions of his brain protruded from the exit wound over his right ear as he crashed into a pew. The pellets from the shotgun blew a chunk off the pew as he fell across it.

Don was up on his feet as fast as the pellets in his side and back would allow him. He stood over Winters. The wounded homicide detective looked up at him not knowing what to expect. He spotted her gun and retrieved it. He ejected the clip and tossed it behind the pews, well out of her reach. He dropped the gun beside her.

"I ain't finta do shit to you," Don said. "So you ain't got to be looking at me all like that."

Winters didn't reply. Her attention was focused on the pistol in Don's hand.

As if to quell her fears he tucked the pistol into his waistband.

"You're under arrest, Donald Haskill," Winters breathed.

"Yeah, sure," Don said as he stepped over her and made his way out of the chapel.

Winters staggered to her feet using a pew to balance herself. She retrieved her gun and the clip from behind the pews and made her way outside. In front of the funeral home there was no sight of Donald Haskill. As she stood holding her ribs a police cruiser slid around the corner and screeched to a halt in front of her.

"Fuck!" Winters screamed into the uncaring night.

DON RETURNED TO THE ABANDONED BUILDING. IT HAD
been harder to get in this time. Heavy construction machinery was blocking the previous route and someone had re-
paired the hole in the chain-link fence. They had also
replaced the board across the hallway. It would have been
easy work to bypass the machinery and pull the board off
the door, but the small, painful holes in his side and back
made the job difficult. He reclaimed his room in the third-
floor apartment. He didn't even know why he came back
here instead of hitting the road. He guessed it had to be because he didn't want to leave his mother in her present condition. He didn't have any idea what he was supposed to do
for her, but he knew he would have to go home one more
time before he left Chicago.

Once again he had been forced to kill. He didn't do it so much to save the lady detective's life as to bring reckoning to one of his sister's murderers. No matter, it was murder just the same.

"Ughhh!" he grunted in pain as he sat on the floor. He closed his eyes and sagged against the wall to get some much-needed rest. He lifted his bloody, ragged shirt and began to pick the shotgun pellets out of his skin. He dropped the bloody pellets on the floor. Blood seeped from the small wounds in his side and back. On his hands the smell of cordite from the gunpowder was strong.

Satisfied that he had removed most of the shotgun pellets, Don closed his eyes and lolled against the wall. Images of his naked mother and dead sister crowded the space behind his eyelids. He watched Johnny's body fall sideways in slow motion. Dre was facedown in the street. Sajak's brains flew into his face as Lonnie tried to shoot him in the face. Diego was on his knees begging for his life. The woman detective looked up at him waiting for him to kill her, too. Juanita ran in front of the truck and her body flew into the air.

Don opened his eyes knowing there would be no rest from the visions of death. He dug through his pockets and pulled out his crack and pipe. The two ounces of crack had dwindled considerably, but there was still a nice-sized piece—maybe a half ounce. With trembling fingers Don packed the pipe bowl with the shake from the bottom of the bag. His first lighter was almost out of fluid, but he had another one. He flicked its powerful flame and waved it across the bowl to melt the chips of crack. Sucking like a vacuum, he pulled the smoke into his lungs until it made him puke.

Vomiting made his wounds hurt even more. To numb himself, Don broke a huge chunk of crack and dropped it in the bowl. He lit it and took a mighty hit.

This time he felt intense pain instead of pleasure. His lungs felt like he had swallowed molten lava. A spasm shook his frail frame like a leaf in a high wind. His nervous system went awry. The pipe slipped from his fingers as Don grabbed his left arm. Foam bubbled at the corners of his mouth. Every tortured breath he pulled into his lungs felt like he was swallowing steel-wool pads. He tried to claw his way up the wall but a pain exploded in his chest making him slide down the wall to his original sitting position. Blood began to mix with the foam dribbling down his chin out of his mouth. His brain felt tight in his skull like it was too big for the cavity. Searing hot daggers spread from his chest as if his blood had been emptied out of his body and replaced with napalm. Don convulsed again as a series of a mini-strokes paralyzed his limbs. He passed out.

When he came to, he didn't know how long he had been out, but he found he couldn't move. As long as he took short breaths, the pain in his lungs was less intense. Gathering his strength, Don tried to call out for help, but his brain couldn't convince his voice to cooperate. It didn't hurt too much to open his eyes so he lay there, watching.

The moon climbed and then dipped. It began to lighten outside as the sun started to shine down on the rooftops of the ghetto. Birds began to chirp, cheerfully unaware of Don's paralysis. With clucks, coos, and whistles they nagged him to get up and start his day. He could hear voices outside of the building now.

Police flashed through Don's head. He whimpered as he tried to move. It was no use, his body was broken. Tears rolled into his eyes and he felt his heart beating mildly but erratically in his chest. The voices weren't in a hurry, though. He managed to calm down enough to try and hear what the unseen men were talking about. The usual authoritative, urgent tone the police used was missing. He could just make out what the voices were saying.

"Knock the sides out on the third floor and then drop that ball on through the roof," someone shouted. "We're already behind schedule. We've got to clear this lot and clear lot seventeen by the end of this month. You lazy son of a bitches! Get that damn hose on and start spraying water on the damn building so the dust don't get too thick for us to see!"

Don felt drops of water coming through the window.

The voice continued, "Okay, Pete! Go ahead and swing that fucking ball!"

Through the open window Don watched the gigantic iron wrecking ball swinging toward the apartment. In his mind he was screaming.

LETTER FROM THE AUTHOR

Peace. I wrote *Slipping* because I wanted to give a face to the numerous victims of illegal narcotics, mainly crack cocaine, in urban America. Conspiracy theorists say that crack was part of the government's plan to destroy the Black community nationwide. That may or may not be true. I don't know if crack was designed to do that, but I know it played a huge part in it. In the late eighties and early nineties, crack cocaine took its toll on many families, whether it was the repercussions of selling it or smoking it. The simple fact is, we weren't prepared for the tidal wave of crack that flooded our neighborhoods. It has been about twenty years since crack made its appearance on our streets, and the toll it has taken has been astronomical. Just the thought of how many prisons have been built because of crack cocaine is mind-numbing.

If you think I'm playing, go to your local municipal court. Have someone point you to drug court and watch the steady procession of dealers and users.

I used to get high. It started off innocently enough at the age of twelve with a puff off a joint and a swig of beer. By the time I quit at the age of twenty, I was smoking crack on weed (premos) in near-lethal doses on a regular basis. I can remember swearing I would never smoke crack in any way, shape, or form. I'll always remember that tweaking, paranoid, exhilarating, nauseating, heart-pounding, guilty feeling that premos would give me, and I pray to Heaven that I never experience that again. I was fortunate never to have grown into a full-fledged rock star, but many of my peers weren't that lucky. Even now, after close to a decade and a half of sobriety, I know I'm always in a precarious position when it comes to chemicals—just one drink or drug away from going back down that road.

I often hear non-users swear up and down that it's simply a mind thing. I don't dispute that, but that's not the whole drug phenomenon. It's a soul thing, too. My uneducated guess is that our individual psychological makeup makes many of us susceptible to drug addiction. We spend countless dollars, hours, and energy trying to self-medicate. As a teenager I often felt lonely, awkward, maladjusted, or unloved. If I had a big bag of weed, some cocaine, raw or cooked, and some champagne with pineapple orange juice, I was good to go. This is not to say that average, everyday, normal people don't get addicted, but I think we fabulously unbalanced people have a greater chance of becoming slaves to narcotics.

I often think about the famous "War on Drugs" and the effect it's had on people. Since the influx of crack cocaine into urban, and later, suburban America, millions, even billions of dollars have been spent on this fictitious war. Once again, politicians spent the taxpayers' dollars to treat the symptoms, not the disease. Those funds would have been better spent building treatment centers, educating our nation about the seriousness and pervasiveness of addiction, bringing affordable mental health care to our communities, and fighting the social and economic conditions in which the crack culture flourished. Utopian-thinking, silly me.

Actually, I support the legalization of narcotics. Don't be taken aback. In certain communities, the stuff is treated like it's legal anyway. If it's legalized it will have the same drawing power as alcohol, and the government could regulate its use (if they don't already). That would remove some of the dangers associated with its use and purchase. Translation: That Fortune 500 vice president will be less likely to walk into Walgreen's and buy an eightball. Bringing a problem like this to light would give society a truthful picture of the American addict and his counterpart, the dealer. This will not happen, because it would bring our legal system to a grinding halt. We wouldn't need half as many judges, lawyers, prisons, prison guards, and police.

When I was still in the streets, every time an addict would walk up to me selling his child's diapers, his aunt's television, or whatever, I would think about the power that drugs have over people. It also made me think about where I would be now if I hadn't gotten some help. While chasing that crack, there's no telling how many people I would have hurt, directly or indirectly. I have to thank my higher power that that isn't my life today.

It seems that the novelty of crack is finally beginning to wear off in our communities, whether because of people getting help to get their lives back, going to prison, or dying. It's not over. I'm not saying that. We have a decade-plus of hard knocks to learn from. The effort to rebuild our communities will have to be like Reconstruction after the Civil War, but it can and must be done. And if another cheap, plentiful, easily accessible drug comes along in this new millennium, I would like to think that we have learned from our mistakes and are better equipped to deal with it. Until next time, y'all.

Peace,
Y. Blak Moore

ACKNOWLEDGMENTS

As always I acknowledge the Creator, the beauty and wonder of our universe, and pray for an end to our depravity and insensitivity.

Tebby, I wish you would gone head and write that book. To my nephews, Dwight, Devin, and Darius.

Since this was an old school joint, I've got to acknowledge some of my old school fools: Tony Cleveland, Billy Will, my cuzo Bre, my cuzo Tanya, my little cuzos (well not so little anymore) Chad and David, Rube, Rajon, Ced, Abdullah, Junior, Vance, Brian and Pokey Peace, Scoots, Boo-Boo, Kwami, Insane Wayne, Jimmy D the King of Sig, Black Keith, Tito (RIP), Big Jerry, Anthony, Mad Max, Big Brew, Morris, Earl, Pooh Dog (RIP), Howard (RIP), Crucial, Rob Base, Big-Bank Hank, Big Martini, P-Funk, Slo-Kid,

G-Craps, Square Biz, Crackdaddy, Leroy, Pete Rose, Big Ray, Lil Essie (RIP Sleeze, love yo punk ass), King Gatty, Keno (Nolan Ryan, much love), Mickey (Mookie), Tanya (Apple-lo), Poobie (Big Al), Toya (Puffy Face), Squirrel, Boogie, Cujo (Nose), Jay, Pooh Man (Thirsty), Lil Bryan (RIP), Plucky Duck, Lil Man, Lil G (both of y'all 510 & 511), T-Man, Bubble-Yum, Chevy (RIP), Gus, Mack, Rat, Pat, Pooh (PG-Slime Thug), Thick Mick, Zonnie (Scoody Woody), Vicky Ma, Nicky Nu, Shahidah, Mary, Keisha, Jermaine (Herm), Terrell (Grimeski, shut up punk), Reggie Clark, Toke, Mike Ski, D-Low, E-ric, Shoemouth (RIP), Ice Dolen, DC, Magic Juan, Mase, Face, Bleek (Mr. Neal), Geo, 50Bill (RIP, I still owe you from that last egg/water fight), Skitback (that what you on?), Biggie, Eddie Delaney, Chill (RIP), Geno (RIP), Cocky Ed, Joe Cool, Big Shorty, Tywan, Shock Diesel, Lil Willis, Big Goon, Rachel (gray-eyed rat, you know I love you), CK, Chickaboo, Marcus Jefferson, Killa Cali, Cheesecake (RIP), Charlie Hines (RIP), Toby Blue, Big Tobe, Big Ant, Super Lou, Dwight, Hunky B, Lawrence, J-Ball, Black Jamie (RIP), Rashawn, Gigolo, Barbeque (Rapping Rodney), Tical, Smallhead, Tubby (RIP), Kemo (RIP), Marty Boo (RIP), Marly Fraud (Fraud Jenkins), D-Mike (Debo), Chuck, Floyd, Whitey (RIP), Murder Mike, Vonnie (I'll still knock you out), Punkin (Got to stay away from your hugs), Talibah (Tally what's up, pimp) Noni (Dimepiece) . . . Whew, that's enough.

If I missed you, I'm sorry. If you can't accept that KMA.

Y. BLAK MOORE

SLIPPING

A READING GROUP GUIDE

QUESTIONS FOR DISCUSSION

The questions and discussion topics that follow are intended to enhance your group's reading of Y. Blak Moore's *Slipping*. We hope they will provide new ways of looking at this insightful novel.

1. The overarching theme of *Slipping* seems to be that using crack is a one-way road to destruction. Do you think Don-Don's story is realistic? Why or why not?
2. Juanita enters Don-Don's life during a basketball game, by chance. And eventually she is the person who convinces Don-Don to smoke crack. Do you think that if he had never met her that he would probably not have ever tried that particular drug? If you think he would have

become a crackhead anyway, discuss why. If you think it was entirely her fault, explain why.

3. Dre is Don-Don's oldest friend and he is the last person who wants to believe that Don-Don is becoming a tweaker. When Don-Don goes after his old crew to get some help hustling, they reject him—and so does Dre. Is this an example of the worst kind of betrayal? Or is there anything wrong with Don-Don's predicament at this point?

4. Rhonda, Don-Don's sister, seems to sense that something is wrong with her baby brother, and Mrs. Haskill, Don-Don's mother, also gets worried when her son disappears for long stretches of time. But neither of the two women ever catch on to how bad things get for Don-Don and what his and Juanita's life is like cooped up in his bedroom. Do you think Don-Don's family should have, or could have, intervened sooner to steer him away from his tragic path? If yes, what could they have done differently?

5. Growing up in the hood is challenging for all of the kids in *Slipping,* and most of the characters in the book make their living off of selling drugs or selling stolen goods. A few people, however, like Rhonda, Don-Don's sister, are determined to get degrees and get jobs and move out. How is it that two kids from the same family (Don-Don and Rhonda) could lead such drastically different lives, with entirely different goals?

6. *Slipping* demonstrates with violent clarity how vicious a street thug has to be in order to survive, but it also

shows how the influx of crack use inside the African American community might have introduced a new kind of desperation for addicts. Do you think the author convincingly portrays what new problems this drug might have produced? How does the author paint the "before-crack" and "after-crack" picture of the hood?

7. Don-Don seems to have little remorse for how he treats Juanita, and doesn't have many qualms about killing any obstacle in his way by the end of the novel. Is this part of Don-Don's innate personality or did the crack do this to him? If you think it's the crack, explain why you think crack motivates Don-Don. If you think he would have turned out like that anyway, explain what motivates Don-Don.

8. In a couple places in the novel, the author states that a Black man is standing on the corner doing what Black men everywhere do: stand on the corner and wait for a hustle. Is this true, and if so, what does it imply about urban African American men? Discuss who is responsible for this situation. If false, explain why the author would make this apparent exaggeration.

9. Is how Don-Don leads his life wrong? If yes, explain why. If no, explain why his actions are justified.

10. Why is it that Don-Don fell victim to crack abuse while his closest friends did not? Does the fact that they didn't become tweakers suggest that crack use didn't sweep the African American community as strongly as the author wants us to believe?

A CONVERSATION WITH
Y. BLAK MOORE

Why did you decide to write about crack use in your third novel?

I thought it was a relevant subject to write about, being that I write for and about the streets, and it wasn't too long ago that crack cocaine was taking us under at an alarming rate. It [the crack epidemic] still isn't over, but we're coming back from it.

Who do you want to read this book and how do you wish them to think about it?

Well, as a writer, I want anyone who wants to read it to pick it up, but mainly the young cats and girls out there who don't really understand what happened to a lot of us during this period in our struggle in America. Also, I don't think that we realize just how much a lot of today's adolescents in the inner city were affected by crack cocaine.

You have three children. Do you discuss your books with them? What have you told them about your past history with drug abuse?
I have two daughters, one fourteen years old, the other thirteen, and a three-year-old son. I talk with my daughters about my books and hope they get something out of them. I have talked with them at length about addiction and addictive personalities, which seem to run in my family.

Some people might see Slipping *as a cautionary tale while others might see it as an exploitation of a serious problem. What would you say to each of these judgments?*
If anyone can see this as being exploitation—simply put—they are a hater, and there's nothing I want to say to them. *Slipping* is purely a cautionary tale, but I couldn't just say, "Do drugs and die!" I had to give them something to latch on to.

You mention in your author note that you think drugs should be legalized. What do you think that would accomplish and do you feel this way about all drugs? Also, you've been sober for many years. Does your desire to see drugs legalized conflict at all with your desire not to use them ever again?
I've been clean and sober for fourteen years now. I know

that legalizing drugs is an age old argument, but I whole heartedly agree that it should be done, especially if the government can't seem to stem the manufacture, distribution, and sales of these illegal substances in our great country. As we saw in the old days, prohibition does not work, instead it spawns a black market for said prohibited substances. Along with these black markets, such things as wholesale violence and a certain degree of lawlessness accompany them hand-in-hand.

If your children wanted to experiment with drugs, would you let them? If yes, at what age? And with what drugs?
No, I would never condone any experimentation with drugs by them at any age. Though I know that one day they will become adults and have the right to make choices in their lives such as drug use, I will still never condone it and they can never do it around me.

A lot of your fans are in prison and feel that you are particularly good at describing "the life" on the streets and in the joint. Do you think people who haven't experienced some of what you write about firsthand will be able to relate to your characters anyway?
Hopefully so, I like to think that I break it down enough for anyone to catch on. I think that the inner city culture has always been sort of a phenomenon to outside cultures and they like to take a peek at the way some of us live. I mean there are billion-dollar examples of this such as hip-hop.

How do you think crack changed the urban African American community? Do you think that if crack hadn't become popular that something else would have caused the same problems or is there something specific about the consequences of using/introducing this drug?

Most definitely, yes. Crack changed the urban African American community. It divided us even more than we were. It turned kids into killers, and killers into kings for a short while. A countless number of my brethren languish behind bars and many a corpse grows moldy in its coffin because of crack cocaine. If it wasn't crack that struck us so hard, it would have been something else because the black race in urban America was waiting on something to assuage our existence. What better than something that could make you feel good or feel rich? As babies of the sixties and seventies our psychological makeup made us easy prey for crack cocaine, a potent mixture of problem-solving, mind-numbing escapism.

Which character in Slipping *do you relate to the most? Say a little about how you are creatively inspired.*

I like to think that I relate to them all because I created them, and that makes them all my children, be they good or bad. I'm usually inspired by the things that ail the people around me—my family, friends, neighborhood, community, city—and crack cocaine during the late eighties and the nineties affected so many of us, it was and is ridiculous.

What is most important to you about slipping? Getting across a message or providing a good, entertaining read? What do you want your readers to take away from this particular book?

I wanted to do both. Like I mentioned before, it wasn't an ad for drug prevention; it's a novel, so it has to be entertaining to some degree. But it also has to have some imagination to make readers want to take the journey with you.

ABOUT THE AUTHOR

Y. BLAK MOORE is a poet and a former gang member who grew up in the Chicago housing projects. He is also the author of *Triple Take* and *The Apostles*. Blak has three children and lives in Chicago. You can reach him via e-mail at yaniermoore@hotmail.com.